I0780206

BACK TO PORT ROYAL

A TIME TRAVEL ROMANCE

LOVE THROUGHOUT TIME
BOOK FIVE

ID JOHNSON

Copyright © 2025 by ID Johnson

All rights reserved.

No part of this book may be reproduced in any form or by any electronic or mechanical means, including information storage and retrieval systems, without written permission from the author, except for the use of brief quotations in a book review.

Book cover by Sparrow Book Cover Designs

https://www.facebook.com/sparrowbookdesigns/

For Riley, my third daughter. You're going places, "my girl."

CONTENTS

RUM AND RUINS

I'm sweating in a polyester corset.

Not a proper, laced-up-with-care historical corset, but a cheap polyester knockoff with faux brass buttons that feel like they might peel off if I breathe too hard, and a faint chemical scent that's becoming harder to ignore the longer it bakes in the sun. The fake leather belt at my waist digs into my ribs every time I shift on the creaky bench of the tour boat. My thighs are glued to the vinyl seat, and my curls are rapidly evolving into a lion's mane of frizz.

If I die of heatstroke before I ever see Port Royal, I want that in my obituary.

Sabrina Torres, 25, museum archivist and occasional bad cosplayer of pirate history, perished tragically while wearing a plastic sword.

"Will you stop fidgeting?" Maddie bumps her shoulder into mine, grinning. "You're ruining the look. Real pirates didn't pout."

"They also didn't have to deal with synthetic fabric in tropical humidity," I mutter, tugging at the laces of my top with fingers already damp with sweat. "This was supposed to be fun, not a slow roast."

"Come on, look at this place!" She gestures out toward the horizon with her drink, some kind of neon slushy swirling in a clear skull-shaped cup, complete with a black bendy straw. "Rum, sun, history... and you, getting to talk about your dead colonists and crumbling pottery."

"Ceramics," I correct automatically. "Glazed redware, to be exact."

She rolls her eyes dramatically and sips her drink. "Says the woman who hasn't had a vacation in two years. And you picked this place."

That shuts me up.

I know she's right. It's been nonstop for months, rotating exhibits, processing funding applications, handling donor events and paperwork, spending late nights and early mornings in the museum's archives, hunched over fading ink and flaking pages. My phone never stopped buzzing, my inbox never dipped below seventy unread messages, and even when I wasn't at work, I was still *obsessively thinking* about work.

New York doesn't feel oceans away. It's only been a couple of days since I stepped away from the museum, and I still feel the ghost of my latest exhibit catalog beneath my fingertips. Maddie had to practically drag me out of the building to get me on the plane, muttering something about "tropical intervention."

I chose Port Royal for the beautiful beaches and the soft spot I've always had for it in my heart. An island that was maimed by an earthquake, and then immediately afterward, a tsunami. How could anyone survive?

So, here we are, because I needed a break, and my boss threatened to "take my ID badge hostage" if I didn't use my PTO.

And, fine, because my ex is now dating someone with a body sculpted by Aphrodite herself and a lifestyle brand called *GlowUp-Academy*.

I needed distance, salt air, rum, and maybe a cute, sun-bronzed, tall, dark, and handsome type fling.

But now I'm here, dressed like Jack Sparrow's cheap floozie cousin on a historical pirate booze cruise with my best friend Maddie. The ocean sparkles like crushed glass. The sky is a postcard-perfect blue, dotted with lazy clouds that drift like sails. A pelican glides low over the water.

Who knows? Maybe it'll actually be fun?

The boat rocks gently beneath us as the guide—a wiry man in a plastic tricorn hat–struts to the bow, waving a dollar-store cutlass. "Now, me hearties," he booms in an exaggerated accent, "ye be sailin' near the cursed waters where the wicked men of the sea once roamed, drinkin' rum and buryin' their treasure!"

"I bet you ten bucks he says 'Davy Jones's locker' before we get back to shore," I whisper out of the side of my mouth.

"Twenty says you'll be correcting his historical inaccuracies before the next island," Maddie shoots back, and I almost smile.

The ruins of the old city come into view, rising from the water like spirits with unfinished business. Broken teeth of stone and barnacle-crusted walls peek through the surf, remnants of a city that defied nature and gods alike. I lean forward, squinting. I see the leaning spire of Fort Charles, tipped like a finger frozen mid-collapse. The jagged outline of what was once a bustling marketplace curls along the shore, half-swallowed by sea and silt.

I know these shapes. I've studied them. Sketches in old journals, grainy underwater photographs taken by divers. This isn't just scenery to me—it's magic.

"I wish we could've seen it back then, before the earthquake," I say. "Even though they rebuilt it, it was never the same as before the storm."

Just for a second, I close my eyes and let my mind fill in the blanks. Red-tiled roofs baking in the sun. The clatter of hooves on stone streets, mingling with shouts in Spanish, English, Portuguese, French, and West African tongues. The stench of fish, gunpowder, sugarcane, and smoke. The chaotic heartbeat of a port city teetering between empire and ruin.

Port Royal wasn't just a pirate haven. It was *alive*—brash, brutal and magnetic. Bursting with stolen gold, fast ships, and faster betrayals. A powder keg of politics and profit. Then, on June 7, 1692, the Earth opened its throat and swallowed half the city whole.

This place was once called the *wickedest city on Earth*. Port Royal was fire, fortune, and rot all sewn together until it sank beneath the sea like a drunkard slipping beneath the waves.

I've read the journals and studied the fault line. I've held a coin fished from a sunken cellar in my gloved hands and cataloged it under soft lighting with obsessive reverence. But now....

Now, I'm floating above it.

A place I've only seen through glass cases and sepia-toned maps is right *there*, whispering just below the surface.

Suddenly, the sweat doesn't matter. The corset, the costume, the heat... none of it matters. This is why I do what I do–the thrill of seeing something real, something impossibly old and impossibly *surviving*, something touched by the hands of the past. No barriers, gloves, or glass. History isn't dead. It's waiting to be rediscovered.

The boat turns slightly, tracing a slow arc along the edge of the submerged ruins. I press my hand to the railing and lean over to get a closer look at a fragment of wall where sea moss has begun to claim the past. For the first time in months, maybe longer, I feel completely alive.

Thunder cracks, loud, sudden, and strong.

I jerk my head up just in time to see the sky turning black—not drifting into clouds like a normal storm, but *devouring* the sky. Shadows crash across the horizon like a door slamming shut. One second it's bright, blue, and breezy. The next, it's night, and the wind is howling.

"Whoa," someone gasps. The tour guide falters mid-sentence, lowering his ridiculous plastic cutlass. His voice wavers. "Storm came outta nowhere—"

No kidding.

The boat pitches sharply. Someone stumbles into me. I barely stay upright as the waves start slamming into the hull.

"Drop anchor!" a crew member yells, real panic in his voice now.

"I said pull the damn sails in, now!" another hollers.

The wind smacks me across the face like it means to split skin. My eyes water, and my hair whips into my mouth. Maddie grabs my wrist, hard.

"Sabrina, what the hell is happening?"

I open my mouth, but before I can answer, a wave crashes over the side, blinding us, cold and violent. My body jerks forward as the boat lists hard to port. Water pours down my back, into my boots. The plastic sword at my side rips loose and disappears into the sea.

The ocean is *roaring*–louder than engines, louder than the people screaming now, louder than anything I've ever heard in my life. My ears ring with it. Someone is crying nearby. Someone else is shouting over the wind, but I can't understand a word. I cling to the bench railing. Maddie's hand slips. She disappears beneath the surface.

Then a wave hits. Not just big—*impossibly huge*. A wall of water the size of a building, rising from the deep like some god-punishment from myth. Everything inside me says run, dive, *do something*, but I can't move.

Water slams into me, filling my mouth and nose. My ribs ache from the force of it. I'm spun like a rag doll, flipped end over end. I don't know which way is up. My arms flail but find nothing. My legs kick, panic taking effect now, full throttle.

I can't breathe. My chest *burns*. Everything is black, cold, and spinning. My lungs seize.

Finally, I break the surface with a choking gasp, coughing, gagging, saltwater spilling from my throat. I blink furiously, trying to see, trying to *breathe*—but all I can taste is salt and bile.

Where's Maddie? I spin. Where's the boat? Where's *anything*?

I'm alone.

There are no bright plastic flags fluttering in the wind. No yelling crew or overacting pirate guide. No tourists laughing... or screaming.

Just sea, dark blue-green and endless. The sky is perfectly clear blue, like nothing had happened. No sign of the storm, and not a single cloud. The wind is gone too, replaced by a soft, eerie hush. My heart pounds so hard I feel it in my teeth.

I turn in a circle, treading water frantically. Every muscle screams. My clothes drag me down, heavy and clinging. I'm spinning. Gasping.

"Maddie?" I scream. "Maddie?!"

Nothing.

"HELLO?! SOMEBODY—!"

My voice bounces back at me. I'm shaking, and salt stings the corners of my eyes. I can barely keep my head above water, I'm so tired already. I blink against the salt burn, still scanning, still kicking.

Then—off in the distance. Land? No—wait. Sails. A ship!

The ship bobs in the distance, but it's not a coast guard boat, or even a modern yacht. This ship has three masts and white sails full with the wind, and a dark wood hull glinting in the sun. There are flags I can't make out, ropes hanging from every beam, and the faint shimmer of gold or brass catching the light.

A *frigate.*

"What the—"

I start swimming, my arms shaking and legs heavy and slow, but I push myself forward with everything I have left. Each stroke is a struggle against the weight of my soaked clothes and rising panic. My eyes lock onto the ship ahead, and I silently hope it's some kind of rescue, a tourist boat coming for me.

As I study the ship, I become increasingly curious. The sails, the rigging, the carved woodwork–it's stunningly authentic. So detailed, so *perfectly* true to a seventeenth-century frigate that it almost takes my breath away. I can't believe someone went to such lengths to build a historically accurate ship for tourists. It looks like it's been plucked straight from a museum or a painting.

I keep kicking, every muscle burning, but the ship doesn't seem to get any closer. The sun beats down mercilessly, drying the saltwater on my face and making my lips crack. My throat is raw from shouting into the emptiness. The ocean stretches out in every direction, vast and merciless, swallowing all sound except the soft slap of water against my arms.

Fear twists tight in my chest. How long have I been out here? Minutes? Hours? My limbs feel like lead, and my vision blurs. I try to steady my breathing, but panic claws at my mind like a wild animal.

Still, I refuse to give up. I keep swimming toward the ship. Maybe someone aboard will see me, hear me, realize I'm drowning out here. Maybe they'll throw a rope and pull me in.

I shout again, my voice cracking. "Help! Please! I'm here!"

The wind carries my plea, but for now, the only answer is the endless ocean and the slow, steady rise and fall of the ship's sails on the horizon.

SIREN OR SPY?

Gabriel

The sharp wind slams against my face, and the tropical sun beats down, as *The Tempest's Vow* cuts through the restless waves between Hispaniola and Port Royal. I stand at the helm, my fingers tight on the wheel and my eyes sharp against the spray. The sea is no friend, not today. The sky churns with bruised clouds, a warning in their deep gray-purple. An angry storm just passed us, and we caught the tail end of it from the south.

"Captain!" Finch's voice cuts through the roar, rough and urgent.

I snap my gaze toward the bow. There, I see a figure thrashing in the swell, half-swallowed by the merciless ocean.

"A woman! Alone!" he yells.

Without hesitation, I bark orders. "Prepare the lines! Lower the yawl! Bring her aboard, men!"

The crew moves like clockwork, a well-oiled machine. The yawl reaches her just as the sea drags her beneath the next wave. I watch as her arms flail, desperate. She's gasping, coughing, and fighting for life.

"Grab her!" I order.

Two men seize her arms, hauling her toward the ship on the yawl.

I'm beside them, reaching out, steadying her as they lift her from the yawl's deck onto ours.

She's lighter than I expect, almost fragile, drenched, shivering, and trembling. Her curls cling to her face, dripping seawater into terrified eyes.

"Easy now," I say, my voice low but firm. "You're safe."

She blinks at me, confusion flickering behind the fear.

"Where... am I?" she croaks, her voice cracked and foreign.

"On *The Tempest's Vow*," I reply, watching every movement. "You're lucky we found you."

She tries to sit up, but I place a hand on her shoulder, halting her.

"Don't try to move too fast." I place my hand on her shoulder. "Captain Gabriel Ashford." I introduce myself.

Her gaze drops, overwhelmed, and she shivers again. I turn to Finch. "Bring blankets, fresh water, and something warm to drink."

As he disappears below deck, I stay by her side. I kneel, trying to meet her eyes without seeming threatening. "Did you get caught in that storm that just passed through here too? What's your name?"

She swallows hard, struggling to form words. "Sabrina. Sabrina Torres."

Her name and accent are foreign, strange, like a song from another world. I want to ask where she's from, but her lips are pale and trembling, and I don't want to upset her even more.

I run a hand through my hair, frustration gnawing at me. I'm not a man given to sentiment, not since I left the Royal Navy, but this woman, this stranger in soaked rags, awakens a twinge of compassion I thought long dead. I don't usually allow foreigners on my ship, but this woman has piqued my curiosity.

I step up onto the quarterdeck, giving her space but keeping her in my line of sight, watching without making it obvious. She looks around the ship with keen eyes, as though she intends to one day build her own.

My first mate, Elias Finch, hands her a blanket and a tin cup, steam rising gently from the tea. I can tell he's introducing himself from the way that he bows his head slightly and offers his hand. She shakes it, her fingers trembling. I study her, but not idly. A man learns to read people quickly at sea, for danger doesn't always wear a sword, and yet, nothing about her makes sense.

She's beautiful, yes, but not in the way of powdered ladies at English courts. There's something exotic about her, earthy and strange. Her skin is a creamy honey brown, smooth as polished teak, though windburn now flushes her cheeks. Her hair hangs in long, soaked curls down her back, waist-length, at least. She lifts her eyes, catching mine for a moment, cautiously watching me back.

She speaks to our cook, Isla, and I eavesdrop. At first, her voice carries that same strange lilt I noticed when we pulled her aboard, clipped and unfamiliar. Certainly not an English accent. Not Spanish or French either, but as Isla leans closer and offers her more tea, the woman clears her throat and starts again.

Only now, she's speaking with what I can only describe as the worst impression of a British accent I've ever heard. It's flat in the vowels, as though she's trying to mimic someone from a play. I narrow my eyes. Odd. Very odd.

She glances my way again and quickly looks down. Her dress, or what's left of it, is a puzzle in its own right. From a distance, one might think it's a corset and petticoat, though unlike any I've ever seen. But up close, the truth of it is laughable. The bodice is made of some strange, shiny material that clings to her damp skin. The corset has no real boning, no structure or sense to it, and the belt strapped around her middle looks more like a costume piece than anything fit for a woman's wardrobe.

I've seen better garments hanging in the windows of dockside taverns, cheap dressings for cheaper women, but there's no filth to her, no slurred speech or wine-stained teeth. Just the silly clothes, and that strange, false accent, and the way her gaze keeps darting over the ship as though she is trying to memorize it. Could she be a spy? But for whom?

Who in God's name is she?

Not a native of these islands, that much is clear. And not one of the merchant class, either. Her hands are too fine for labor, too soft for years at sea.

Finch sidles up beside me, his arms crossed. He follows my gaze and makes a face like he's swallowed a rotten fig.

"She doesn't belong here," he mutters. "I don't like her."

"She was drowning," I answer, keeping my tone level. "Whether she belongs or not, the sea would've taken her."

Finch scowls. "Maybe the sea meant to."

I ignore him.

The woman, Sabrina, lifts the cup to her lips and sips. She closes her eyes, relief washing over her features for just a heartbeat.

It strikes me then how fragile she looked when we hauled her aboard, and yet somehow, she'd survived that storm alone. No boat, crew, or driftwood–just her, floating in the damned channel.

Who survives something like that?

I walk over to her, watching her carefully. She opens her eyes, startled.

"Feeling better?" I ask.

She nods, grateful and wary all at once. "Yes. Thank you, Captain."

The fake accent again is somehow *worse* now. I don't let my expression shift, but I feel the suspicion curl tight in my gut.

"I imagine you've got quite a tale to tell," I say quietly.

She nods and sips her tea slowly, wrapped in damp wool, and I can see she's exhausted. That's what keeps me from pressing her with questions. That, and the tremor I still see in her hands. The sea stole the heat from her bones, and she's shaking, from fear and cold. She's not a threat, not in her current state.

I glance toward Isla, who's watching Sabrina the way she watches stray cats: half skeptical, half softhearted. She'll take care of her.

"Miss Torres," I say, offering her my hand to help her stand. "Come. Let's get you out of those wet things before they freeze to your skin."

She blinks, surprised. "I beg your pardon?"

"You're half-drowned and trembling. Isla'll take you below, find you something dry. Nothing fancy, but it'll keep you warm."

Sabrina nods slowly, her voice soft. "Thank you."

Isla steps forward before I can even call her name. "This way," she says, taking the woman by the elbow like it's her own idea. "Let's find something that doesn't smell like dead fish."

Sabrina gives a faint huff of laughter, and then she's gone, following Isla down into the belly of the ship. I stand there a moment longer, staring after them.

"She's peculiar," Finch says at my shoulder.

I don't jump. Of course he's there, quiet as rot and twice as unwelcome. "I didn't say she wasn't," I reply.

"She's lying."

"About? She didn't say anything yet."

"Exactly."

I sigh and start toward the companionway. "Follow."

We step below deck, down a ladder worn smooth by years of salt and boot leather. The low ceiling creaks with the sway of the ship. I open the door to my quarters and walk inside.

The captain's study is small, but solid. Wood-paneled walls, a broad desk scattered with charts, and a narrow porthole with the sea sliding past outside. It smells of ink, salt, and smoke, familiar and grounding. Finch closes the door behind us.

"Well?" I ask. "You clearly have opinions."

"She's no castaway. You saw what she was wearing." He's emphatic.

"I saw," I say. "Some kind of strange imitation or costume, cheap and stiff. I'm not certain… perhaps she's wearing borrowed clothes? Where do you think she came from?"

"I've never seen silk that looked like that. Or brass for that matter. Her boots with strange seams, and the accent?" He scoffs. "You've heard theater girls try to pass for gentry before. They're better at it. Do you think she's a spy?"

I meet his gaze. "I certainly intend to find out."

He paces, stiff and bristling. "We're two days from Port Royal, and you're harboring something we can't explain. What if she's a hex? A curse? A sea-witch?"

"She didn't bring that storm."

"You don't know that."

"She didn't flinch when we pulled her out. She didn't cry or scream. The girl looked as though she were memorizing the ship."

"That's what's strange!" Finch slams a hand down on the desk. "You bring aboard a strange woman with strange clothes and even stranger speech, and now you're treating her like some royal guest."

"She's not a guest," I say calmly. "She's a mystery, but she's not a threat. Not yet."

He glares at me for a long moment, then backs away with a grunt. "You're going soft."

I laugh and excuse Finch from my quarters. The very idea of going soft is humorous to me, our mission being that of revenge.

He opens the door but pauses. "Mark me, Ashford, women don't just wash up on your deck like mermaids."

The door shuts behind him, and I sit there in silence for a long moment, staring at the sea through the porthole. She's not common, of that I'm certain.

I lean back in the chair, the old wood groaning beneath me. The sun's lower now. The light slants amber, casting long, flickering lines across my desk and the weather-stained charts scattered on its surface.

Finch isn't wrong. Strange things don't happen without reason out here. The ocean has a mind of its own, and I've lived through enough storms to know not all of them come from the sky. Some blow in wearing armor. Some arrive with a sword at your throat. And some… wear corsets made of something that isn't quite leather. Still, I've made worse choices than rescuing a half-drowned woman.

Much worse.

I wasn't always a privateer. There was a time I stood on the deck of a Royal Navy ship, my uniform crisp and boots polished, speaking orders with a spine stiffened by duty and family name. Lieutenant Gabriel Ashford, son of Lord Edwin Ashford of Essex. The second son, the spare.

It's easy to forget that I was ever clean-shaven and proper, fed by silver spoons and sharpened by academy masters with royal pride. Alas, it's all still in me, somewhere beneath the scars and salt.

I joined the Navy at fifteen, desperate to prove I was more than a younger son. My brother, James, was the heir, taller, kinder, better spoken, better liked. I didn't begrudge him. He was a good man, and I loved him.

And then the Spanish took him. Set fire to his ship in the Gulf, no warning, no mercy. The flames lit the horizon for miles, or so I was told. They left nothing behind but a few blackened timbers adrift on the tide.

After that, I stopped believing in orders, in kings and courts that let men die for trade routes, land, and gold. I deserted two weeks later, and have been at sea ever since.

The Tempest's Vow came into my hands the way most ships do—through blood and fire. She was French when I found her, bleeding from the hull, her sails ripped like ghosts. I patched her up, gave her a new name and a new purpose. We've been together ever since.

Now, I sail under a letter of marque when it suits me, and ignore it when it doesn't. The Crown turns a blind eye as long as my cannon stays aimed at their enemies, but I don't serve them. Not truly. I serve my crew and my ship.

Yet, something about that woman—the way she looked at us, bothers me. People who fear death cling to anything, but she wasn't clinging. She was observing, like she'd fallen from the sky and expected to find this ship waiting for her. She wasn't screaming or crying, as any English noble lady would have after being pulled aboard a pirate ship. Rather, Sabrina was memorizing the rigging. What kind of woman does that?

I rub a hand across my jaw and glance toward the door. Whatever she is—spy, madwoman, mermaid, or siren—I'll get to the truth.

SALTWATER AND SECRETS

The floor sways beneath my feet like I'm standing on the spine of some enormous creature, its breath rolling beneath the wood. Every surface creaks and groans. The walls lean in slightly, the ceiling feels too low, and the narrow ladder I've just descended opens into a hallway bathed in candlelight. Not the warm, faux flicker of battery-powered ambiance or the dim hum of emergency backup bulbs–real wax and flame. The scent of it curls into my nose—faintly smoky, threaded with tallow.

Isla moves ahead, leading me deeper into the belly of *The Tempest's Vow*, her skirts swaying, her voice trailing behind her. "Mind your step. The boards warp near the galley door."

I nod, still shivering despite the blanket wrapped around me. Everything smells of saltwater, pitch, and smoke, and the air down here is damp. This is not a themed boat ride, or some immersive historical experience with costumed actors and Bluetooth speakers playing sea shanties through hidden wall mounts.

This is real.

The moment the thought crystallizes in my mind, my knees wobble. I press a hand to the wall—wood, rough-hewn and slick with salt—trying to steady myself. I'm beginning to hyperventilate, but I can't afford to panic. Not here. Not now.

Because the captain—the man with storm-gray eyes and a voice like velvet—is suspicious of me, and my terrible British accent. His first mate already scowls at me, and Captain Ashford might be kind enough to rescue a stranger, but he's not stupid. He knows there's something different about me.

So I take a few deep breaths because I don't want to draw any more attention to myself than I already have. I need to blend in.

The floorboards *are* warped and uneven, just like Isla said. The doorways are tiny, some lashed closed with iron latches instead of knobs. There's no hum of electronics or engine vibration beneath the deck. No buzz of fluorescent lights, no hiss of running plumbing. Just the slap of the sea against the hull and the quiet, low drone of voices above.

Isla's blouse is linen, laced at the wrists. Her skirt is thick, uneven at the hem, and stained with what looks like flour and fish guts. I see no zippers or elastic, and everything she wears looks handmade. Her boots are worn to the shape of her foot, leather cracked with age and use.

And the men... there were no plastic buckles, no Velcro. Their shirts were real homespun linen. Their pants were patched. Some men were barefoot, some with heavy-soled boots nailed into place. They all had knives tucked into sashes at their hips.

I brush a hand over my corset—if you can even call it that. The plastic boning is bent now from the sea, and the cheap polyester sticks to my ribs. It's all wrong, and I hope they didn't notice, but if I were a captain, I'd be suspicious of me.

"Here." Isla stops in front of a small cabin, pushing the door open with her hip. The hinges squeal. "It's the cook's berth, but there's enough space. I'll bring you something clean."

The room is cramped, with two low cots, a trunk in the corner, and a shelf lined with tins and hand-poured candles. There's a single porthole above the cot, crusted with salt.

She turns to me, softening. "You all right, love?"

"Yes," I answer, and this time I try the accent again. "Quite all right, thank you."

She arches her brow, but she doesn't call me on it. Instead, she nods, stepping away. "Right. You get warm. I'll be back with some of my clothes, something that doesn't look like it was made by a drunk tailor with a grudge."

She disappears, and I'm left with my thoughts.

I can't breathe down here, and my hands won't stop shaking. My mouth tastes like salt. I'm not just on an ancient ship....

I'm not in 2025 anymore.

The door creaks open again, and Isla steps inside, carrying a small stack of folded garments and a steaming mug cradled in one hand.

"They're clean, yet a bit rough," she says, setting the clothes down on the edge of the cot.

"Thank you. I'm not particular," I reply, my accent smoother now. Less clipped. Less *American*. I wrap my tongue around the words carefully, rounding the vowels in my mouth like I've been speaking them my whole life. "I just need to get warm."

She gives me a curious look, not suspicious exactly, but like she's trying to figure out who I am, and hands me a second mug of steaming tea.

I take the mug from her hands. It smells like ginger and cloves, and the first sip burns a trail of heat down to my bones.

"Take your time," Isla says, stepping back toward the door. "I'll wait outside."

When the door clicks shut, I sag onto the edge of the cot, my whole body shivering. The tea sloshes in the cup, spilling a few drops. I take another sip, deeper this time, and close my eyes.

Get warm. Get dry. Figure out the rest later.

I set the mug on the floor and peel off the drenched corset and skirt, wincing as the soaked fabric pulls away from my skin. I wrap myself in the wool blanket while I examine the clothes Isla lent me.

The blouse is simple—white linen, with drawstring ties at the neck and sleeves. The skirt is heavy, a faded blue with stitched patches. The undergarments are plain cotton, worn soft with use, with no tags or synthetic fibers.

These aren't costumes. These are lived-in.

My panic pulses harder, but I shove it down and begin dressing. The clothes scratch a little against my skin, but they're warm. When I catch a glimpse of myself in the smudged brass mirror nailed to the far wall, I barely recognize the woman staring back.

Wet curls frizz around my face in a wild, tangled halo. The blouse hangs off one shoulder, the skirt pooling around my legs. I look like a barmaid in a period drama. But the clothes are warm and they fit. I draw in a steady breath.

Just keep going.

There's a knock at the door, and Isla peeks her head in. "Are you dressed, miss?"

"Yes," I say, adjusting the neckline of the blouse.

She steps in, smiling. "Not bad. You could pass for one of us now. Come on, someone wants to meet you."

Before I can ask, she beckons me to follow. I gather my nerves, smooth the front of my skirt, and step into the hallway.

A boy waits just outside the door, maybe sixteen or seventeen, wiry and tan, with sharp cheekbones. His eyes meet mine, curious and cautious.

"This is my brother, Tomas," Isla says. "He's the cabin boy on the ship."

The boy nods politely. "Good day, miss."

"It's nice to meet you both. I'm Sabrina," I say, slipping back into my makeshift accent.

"Where'd your ship go down?" he asks. "You come from the east or the south?"

My mouth goes dry. "I... I'm not sure. Everything happened so fast. One moment I was aboard, and the next there was a storm. I must've hit my head. I don't remember much after that."

A partial truth and believable lie.

Isla studies me, her gaze thoughtful but not accusing. "You don't carry yourself like a maid," she says. "Or a merchant's wife."

I summon a shaky smile. "My father was an officer… in the navy. We were traveling to Port Royal. I didn't expect to end up ship-wrecked."

Tomas cocks his head. "A lady traveling alone?"

"Not alone," I say, eyes flicking down. "I was with my father. There were others, but I… I haven't seen any of them since the wreck. I don't know if—"

I stop myself, letting the grief tighten my throat. That part, at least, doesn't need acting. For the first time, I really stop and allow myself to consider the fact that Maddie may not have made it through the storm, and I have to force back tears.

Isla softens. "Then you're lucky we found you. These waters aren't kind."

I nod, swallowing hard. "I'm grateful. Truly."

They exchange a look, and I glance around again—at the lantern, the riveted beams overhead, the creak of the ship's hull. My mind races. I need answers. A year. A map. *Something.*

But I smile like I belong here. Until I figure out how to get back, I have to survive in the world I just fell into.

The air below deck turns thick and fast. Damp wood, oil smoke, and the ever-present tang of salt make my stomach roll in waves. After only a short time, the warmth I'd longed for begins to smother.

"I need—air," I manage to say, pressing the back of my hand to my mouth.

Isla catches my arm and nods knowingly. "Come on. The decks could use a sweep, and Tomas has been dodging the ropes again. You don't have to help us. You can sit and rest. Just don't get on the first mate's bad side. Elias Finch. He means well, but he can be a bit of a crab."

"Seems as though he's already made his mind up about me," I reply. " He brought me a blanket and shook my hand, but he told me that if I brought darkness onto the ship with me, I could walk off the plank with it."

Isla rolls her eyes. "Finch is mostly bark, less bite. Don't take him too seriously."

We climb the ladder one at a time, the wood groaning under our weight. The second I step onto the main deck, my lungs expand with relief. The open sky, the slap of wind, even the sting of salt air—it's all dizzying, yet welcome.

I press my hand to the railing, steadying myself as the ship rocks. The sun has climbed higher now, casting golden light across the sea. Gulls call overhead, and the crew moves in a strange rhythm around us, men tying down barrels, checking lines, and barking instructions. It feels like a film set, impossibly detailed and alive. Only, I'm the prop that doesn't belong.

I turn to Isla. "I can help," I say.

"Oh no, Miss Sabrina. I can't have you helping. You're a guest aboard the ship."

I don't want to just stand around while everyone else works. "I insist."

"If you're certain, Miss, you can start with these buckets," Isla says gently, handing me a brush. "You'll find seawater works best. Try not to slip."

Isla drops another bucket of seawater near me, sloshing it over the deck. "Watch your knees," she says with a quick smirk. "Salt stings."

"I'm learning that," I mutter, wringing out the brush.

"You get used to it," she says. "We grew up around ships. Our father was a navigator—back in Lisbon."

My head snaps up. "You're from Portugal?"

"Aye," she says, proud and plain. "Born and raised. Tomas too. We've been aboard one ship or another since we could walk."

I nod, wiping sweat from my brow. "That's... incredible."

Isla shrugs again. "It's life. The sea doesn't care where you come from."

But I do. Every new detail spins my head faster. Lisbon, Portugal, navigators. The more I learn, the more impossible this all feels. I drop to my knees and start scrubbing near the rail. Tomas swings a mop lazily nearby, singing something in Portuguese under his breath.

"Keep up," he teases me. "At this pace, we'll reach Port Royal before you finish one board."

I grin, playing along. "Forgive me. I'm not used to this sort of labor."

"Bet you've never swabbed a day in your life."

The sound of boots on the stairs makes us all pause. Captain Ashford doesn't look like any museum portrait I've ever seen of a Royal Navy officer. No powdered wig, no stiff blue coat with polished buttons and gold trim.

No, Captain Ashford must be a privateer. His shirt is loose at the collar, open just enough to reveal a scar along his collarbone and the edge of a tattoo that disappears beneath the fabric. The coat he's wearing is long and battered, made of worn leather that hangs perfectly from his broad shoulders. His boots are scuffed and stained with salt, his belt slung low with a cutlass at his hip and a pistol tucked behind it. No epaulets, no medals, just tools for survival. His dark hair is tied back loosely, strands escaping to frame his handsome, sun-tanned face. His jaw is shadowed with stubble, and his grey eyes are smoldering.

He scans the deck once, pausing when his gaze lands on me. "Miss Torres," he says, his voice smooth. "You're looking more lively." Then, turning to Isla, he asks, "Why are you making her scrub the deck? Is she being punished for something?"

"I offered to help," I reply, standing quickly. "The air below deck… it wasn't agreeing with me."

"Ah, something you'll never get used to, I'm afraid," he says, arms folding as he walks toward us. "It's good to see you feeling better. I take it Isla's been looking after you?"

"She's been more than kind."

His eyes move to her briefly, a faint nod of approval, then back to me. I feel like he's weighing every word I say. Measuring me, and testing my story for cracks.

"I find work clears the mind," I say, and my accent is so good now it startles even *me*… proper vowels, softened R's.

Ashford watches me over the rim of his cup, the wind tugging at the dark curls that have come loose from his tie.

"And where are you from, Miss Torres?" he asks casually.

I force a polite smile. "England, but I grew up all over. My father's in the Navy… or he was. He was on the ship I was on when the storm blew up." I correct myself quickly, hoping the vague answer buys me space and time. "I'm not sure if he made it back aboard the ship or not."

His brow lifts slightly. "I do hope you find him when we dock in Port Royal," he says. "Hmm, Torres?" he adds. "I would've thought you were Spanish."

I blink. *Spanish? Of course.* I curse myself silently.

"Oh, well–" I fumble with a laugh that feels like it belongs to someone else. "My mother's family's English, my father's people originally came from Spain."

He nods slowly, not pushing, but still watching me too closely.

Inside, I groan. Spanish. Why didn't I give myself a Spanish accent? That would've made far more sense with my name, but no, the moment I heard his crisp British tone, my brain panicked and defaulted to mimicking it like a parrot in distress.

Brilliant, Sabrina. Just brilliant.

Unfortunately, Captain Ashford's shadow is quickly joined by a second one. Elias Finch, first mate, leans on the railing with all the blatant arrogance of a man who's decided not to trust me and is going to enjoy every second of it. His dark eyes rake over me with a kind of disdainful amusement.

"Well, well," he says. "She scrubs floors now. What next? Hoisting sails? Climbing rigging?"

"Only if you insist," I say lightly, meeting his stare. "Though I doubt I'd do it half as well as you."

He snorts. "Careful, lass."

Ashford gives him a look sharp enough to cut rope. "Enough, Elias. I'm certain you've business to attend to."

Finch holds his gaze for a beat and walks off with that same insolent swagger. I exhale slowly, gripping the scrub brush tighter.

"Forgive him," the captain says, his voice low enough only I can hear. "He sees ghosts where there are none, but he's loyal, which is hard to replace."

"I understand," I say, which is a lie, but a necessary one.

The captain hesitates another moment, then says, "We'll be reaching Port Royal within a day or two." He tips his hat once, then walks back toward the helm.

I stare after him, my heart hammering and thoughts racing. I need answers soon, or a way out before someone finds holes in my story I can't patch.

The sun dips lower, casting long shadows across the deck. The crew busies themselves with ropes and repairs, their boots thudding against wood, their voices rising in bursts of rough laughter and low curses in more languages than I can track.

Isla appears at my elbow, wiping her hands on her apron. "I could use a hand in the galley, if you don't mind the heat," she says with a crooked smile. "It's not glamorous, but feeding this lot is half the battle."

I nod, grateful for something to do other than scrubbing the deck. "Of course. I'm happy to help."

And I am—sort of. Movement and tasks might help lessen my anxiety.

I follow her belowdecks, into the sweltering little galley tucked near the ship's belly. It smells of garlic and broth. The clatter of pots and the chop of a knife against wood make it feel almost normal. Familiar. Like a kitchen anywhere.

As I chop root vegetables beside Isla, my mind spins beneath the surface like a riptide.

Is Maddie okay? Was she pulled out of the water too? Is she alive? Safe? Still floating somewhere, still hoping someone will see her and pull her aboard?

How do I get back? I don't know how I got here, so how do I reverse it?

And if Maddie is still out there, somewhere in 2025, or the Caribbean, or some liminal space between—how do I find her?

I look down at the strange, borrowed clothes on my body.

I don't belong here.

Yet, for now, I can't fall apart. I have to stay calm, blend in, stay useful, and ask the right questions—subtly, quietly.

This ship is dangerous. These men are dangerous. Gabriel Ashford may have saved my life, but I saw the way he looked at me. He's suspicious, and his first mate is even more so. If I slip, if I say the wrong thing, they'll know.

So I smile as Isla nudges my elbow and tosses me a bunch of herbs to chop. I stir the pot, and focus on the scent, the steam, and the steady warmth of the stove.

But inside, I am screaming.

Maddie, hold on, wherever you are! I'm going to find a way back. I swear!

TELL ME LIES

The galley is too warm for my liking, but I take my usual place at the long bench along the side wall, nodding to Isla as she ladles dinner into battered tin bowls. The crew trickles in, loud and hungry, jostling and jeering, but quieter than usual tonight. It's the girl.

Sabrina.

She sits nearby, her posture too straight for someone used to hard benches. Her hands are steady around the bowl, but she hasn't eaten much.

I can't make sense of her. At first, I thought she might be daft, washed ashore, concussed, babbling in that odd accent of hers. It wasn't quite English, not quite anything. Too stiff, too sharp, but now, hours later, she speaks like one of us. Nearly perfectly, enough to make me doubt my memory.

I chew slowly and study her over the rim of my bowl. She holds herself like someone who's always been in control and is too disoriented to admit she's otherwise. Perhaps she's a noblewoman playing at modesty, or a thief playing at innocence.

She catches me staring and meets my gaze head-on. There's no flinch in her, no demure drop of the eyes. Just that fire again, the one

I saw when she spoke back to Finch, sharp and questioning. There's defiance in it, yes, like she's not afraid of me.

I lean forward, elbows on the table. "You planning to eat that or just admire it?"

She blinks, then smirks faintly. "I'm not used to dinner that bites back."

I raise a brow. "That's Isla's seasoning. She believes the spices hide the smell."

She takes a careful bite, swallows, and says, "I'd say it's doing the opposite."

Around us, the crew laughs, and even Tomas grins behind his spoon. Sabrina smiles too, her gorgeous eyes twinkling.

I wait until the noise settles, then say quietly, "Just so as not to catch you by surprise, we'll be docking at Port Royal within two days. You'll disembark there."

Her spoon pauses halfway to her mouth. "Oh?"

"No offense, Miss Torres, but you're not crew, and you're not cargo," I say, keeping my voice low enough that only she can hear. "You're not anyone's guest, either. You're an unknown, and I don't usually keep an unknown onboard."

She sets the spoon down gently, keeping her composure. "I understand."

She might just be afraid of something after all. I can see it in the way her jaw tightens, the way her shoulders lift just a little too high. She's trying to keep the mask in place, but it's cracking around the edges.

"I appreciate your help," she says, and her accent is still flawless, polished, and... believable. I detect nothing off about it now. "I know I'm a burden."

There it is again–that neat, rounded English. No trace of the strangeness I heard this afternoon. Either I imagined it, or she's learned to mimic us with frightening speed. I don't answer right away. I just watch her.

She's not a castaway, not really. A merchant's wife or daughter wouldn't have reflexes like hers, tense and alert, like someone used to danger. The way she lied was smooth. Not well-practiced, but instinctive. Maybe Finch is right. Maybe she is a mermaid or a sea witch.

I sip my rum, then lean back. "You'll stay in the cook's berth until we dock," I say. "You'll eat, sleep, and keep your head down."

Sabrina nods.

Some part of me wants to believe she's just a lost girl, broken and brave, holding herself together with spirit and stubbornness. Part of me believes she's hiding something far stranger than a noble name or a lover in some port. There's something off about her, and until I know what it is, I'll be watching.

After the evening meal, Elias finds me on the quarterdeck after sundown, perched on a coil of rope with a chipped flask in hand. The stars are just starting to show, and the moon paints a silver path across the water. The wind's fallen to a lazy breeze, and the sails creak like old bones overhead.

"You've been brooding," Elias says.

I offer him a drink. "That obvious?"

He takes a long swig. "It's the girl," Elias says, scratching at his jaw. "She's up to no good."

I glance down at the deck where Sabrina was earlier, scrubbing beside Isla and Tomas like she belonged. She's below now, curled up in the cook's berth with a borrowed blanket.

"She's bizarre, yes," I say evenly. "But not a threat."

Elias snorts. "You don't know that."

I look at him. Elias Finch has been with me through mutinies, storms, and blood-soaked docks. He doesn't spook easily.

"She could be a spy," he says flatly. "Spanish. Or worse—English crown. They're sniffing around again. You know that. Maybe she's been sent ahead to watch, to listen."

"She washed up in rags," I remind him. "Half-drowned." I roll the flask between my palms. "And what? You think she conjured a storm to land herself on our deck?"

"Of course not, but I think she's lying. About all of it." He rises to his feet slowly, the ship rocking gently beneath us. "And I think you're letting your interest blind you."

I clench my fists. "Watch your words."

He meets my stare, steady as ever. "You're not stupid, Ashford, but she's a distraction. And distractions get us killed."

"She's alone," I say. "And if she's lying, we'll find out soon enough."

"Not if we wait too long. What if someone's coming for her?" Elias's voice drops. "Port Royal's not safe. You know that."

"I know," I mutter.

Elias presses on. "You think it's a coincidence she shows up just before we dock? You think her being aboard won't raise questions in port?"

I sigh, dragging a hand down my face. "You want me to toss her overboard?"

"I want you to stop thinking with your gut and start thinking like a captain."

The words sting more than I let on. I've been watching her *too* closely, listening *too* carefully. And for the wrong reasons. That rebellious fire in her eyes, that strange dignity—she pulls at something in me I can't name.

"I told her she's disembarking in Port Royal," I say.

Elias nods. "Good. Then let's keep it that way."

A long silence stretches between us. The sails snap gently above. Below deck, laughter rises, muffled and fleeting.

Finally, I say, "We'll keep eyes on her until then. No wandering. No secrets."

"I already told Isla. She's watching too."

We stand in silence again, staring out over the black water. Somewhere ahead, Port Royal waits—I can feel it already, the tension coiling in my gut.

"She's not the only danger," Elias mutters as he walks to the ladder. Before he climbs down to turn in for the night, he adds, "Think like a captain."

The ship groans, shifting gently with the waves. Most of the crew has turned in. Only a few lanterns burn now, dim glowing halos against the dark. I should be sleeping, but my blood is too hot for rest.

Within the week, we'll strike a Spanish galleon, fat with sugar, gold and silver, sailing north from Cartagena. I've waited two years for this prize. I tracked her course, bribed dockhands and drunk officials, followed whispers through port cities, and now she's within reach.

My hand closes around the rail, my pulse hammering with anticipation. The galleon belongs to a Castilian merchant house, the same house whose crest flew the day my brother's ship was swallowed by cannon fire and sea.

I was too far away to save him, and now... now the gods deliver me vengeance.

But the timing is too perfect, too clean. I glance toward the ladder, where below deck, she sleeps, *if* she's sleeping.

Sabrina Torres, a Spanish name.

It could be nothing. Admittedly, the colonies are full of mixed bloodlines. English mothers and Iberian fathers, of names carried across oceans and woven together by war, blood, and time. But so close to the eve of this attack? A girl with no ship, no story, and no memories floats into my path with a name that rings of Spain, pride, and gold? I'd be a fool not to question it.

She says she was shipwrecked. She says her father served in the navy, but her hands are soft, her manner so very odd.

I rub the back of my neck, restless. There's a storm coming, and I don't mean wind and rain. Is she a spy? Sent ahead to soften us? To gather intel on the crew, the ship, and our plans?

Or is she simply what she claims: a survivor, lost and battered? I close my eyes. Her face comes to me unbidden.

That defiant chin. The way her wet curls clung to her cheek when we pulled her from the sea. The defiance in her hazel eyes when she lied to my face without so much as a tremble.

And she's dangerously beautiful with her impossibly supple skin and perfect lips. The curves of her body are... irresistible.

But she's lying. That much is certain. I should have her locked below. I should tie her hands and force the truth from her lips. Alas, I didn't pull her aboard to hurt her, and when I look at her, some part of me refuses to believe she means us harm. She doesn't have the eyes of a killer.

Perhaps I'm too close. Perhaps her beauty's blinding me to something obvious. If she's connected to that galleon—if she's sent from the same bastards who took my brother from me—then mercy be damned. I'll cut her loose without blinking.

But if she's innocent… God help me. I might already be in too deep, and I don't have the luxury of distractions or mistakes.

Not with vengeance in my sights.

STRANGERS AND STORIES

The sea never stops moving.

Even below deck, with walls around me and wood beneath my feet, the constant sway pulls at my balance, like the ship is trying to remind me that I don't belong, that I'm a passenger in a world that wasn't meant for me.

I sit on the narrow cot, my knees drawn up, a blanket wrapped tight around my shoulders. The wool itches, and the salted air stings my throat. My fingers tremble around the tin cup Isla gave me—ginger tea, she said. It's gone lukewarm now, but I sip anyway, hoping it helps.

Above me, the groan of timber and the thud of boots rattle through the ceiling. Shouting echoes faintly down the ladder well. It's all a blur of noise and motion. I close my eyes, breathing slowly. I can't afford to cry yet, not when I'm already a curiosity. To them, I'm a potential threat.

The captain's made it clear—I'll be gone at the next port. No one's said the word spy, but I can feel it in the silence. The way some of the crew look at me–too sharp, and far too long. The door creaks, and I jolt upright, my heart thudding. But it's only Isla.

"Brought another blanket," she says. "You never know if the night breeze will be hot or cool."

I force a grateful smile. "Thank you. Truly."

She sets the blanket down and eyes me for a second before sitting beside me on the edge of the cot.

"You're scared." It's not a question.

I nod, swallowing hard. I don't know what being left in Port Royal to fend for myself will be like. I don't have a place to stay there, and I don't know anyone. No home, no friends or family waiting—

Isla pulls a small flask from her apron pocket. She offers it. "Rum helps."

I hesitate, then take a tiny sip, and it burns all the way down. I cough, and she laughs softly. "You'll get used to it."

"I don't know if I'll ever get used to this," I admit, staring at the scuffed floorboards. "Any of this."

"It may take a while." Isla shrugs, casual but kind. "It's not easy, and it's definitely difficult being one of the only women aboard. They'll test you, but they'll respect you if you hold your ground."

"I don't know how long I can pretend I'm not terrified."

"Don't pretend," she says simply. "But don't shrink, either. You've got a spine—I saw it the minute you spoke to Elias like you weren't afraid of him."

I laugh weakly. "I was terrified."

She grins. "Still, you held your own. That counts around here."

A knock on the door cuts through the moment, and then a mop of brown hair pokes in.

"Got that rope untangled," Tomas says, addressing Isla. Then his gaze shifts to me, and he offers an awkward smile. "Evening, Miss."

"Evening," I echo.

Isla stands and tousles his hair. "This one thinks he's grown, but he still asks me to stitch his shirts."

"Truly, you're better at it," Tomas snaps, but there's no heat in it. Only familiarity.

They bicker for a moment, teasing, then Isla turns to me. "He'll watch your back when I can't. Won't you, Tom?"

He nods, serious now. "We look after our own."

Our own. It's a simple phrase, but their kindness touches my heart.

After Tomas leaves, Isla turns to me. "You want to survive on this ship?" she says. "Then listen closely. Port Royal's not a safe haven. Everyone wants something—gold, power, revenge. And Captain Ashford...." Her voice drops. "He plays a dangerous game. Smarter than most, but not untouchable."

I meet her gaze. "You trust him?"

She hesitates. "I trust he has his reasons."

Not exactly comforting.

"Elias?" I ask.

She chuckles. "That one? Loyal to a fault, but like I said, don't get on his bad side. He bites."

I manage a small smile. "I think he already hates me."

"Perhaps," she says. "Or he's just trying to figure out who you are, same as everyone else."

I lower my eyes. "I don't even know who I am right now."

Isla crosses the room and sets a bundle of clothes beside me. "Then figure it out before someone else decides for you."

She pauses in front of her cot, opposite mine. "Look strong, even when you're not. We'll keep watch. Now sleep—while you can." And then she crawls into bed, snoring before I even realize she's fallen asleep.

Isla and Tomas are good people, but I'm still a stranger. Still adrift, but maybe I'm not entirely alone.

I stare at the bundle of clothes Isla gave me, brushing my fingers across a seventeenth century, hand-stitched hem. I've seen garments like this before, only they were behind glass.

At the museum, I cataloged pieces like this with cotton gloves and acid-free paper. I've spent years hunched over storage drawers and old ledgers, preserving buttons and petticoats for future generations to admire, and now I'm wearing them, living inside the history I used to curate.

I breathe in the scent of seawater, oil, and stew, heavy in the ship's wooden bones. I don't need a display label to tell me this isn't a replica. This isn't Williamsburg or some immersive maritime theater with enthusiastic re-enactors. This is the real thing, and I'm lost in it.

Still damp and exhausted, I pull the blanket tighter around my shoulders and rest my head against the creaking wall. My stomach aches with dread.

Where are you, Maddie?

I close my eyes. I can still see her fingers slipping from mine, her face going under water. Was she pulled out, too? Did the storm fling her somewhere else? Another century, another ship? Is she alive, calling for help on some foreign coast—or worse, still out there floating....

I sit up quickly, the sudden rush of fear and guilt like a slap.

No. Maddie's tough. We grew up in Brooklyn, after all. No matter what it takes, I have to find my way back to her, but first, I have to figure out where—*and when*—I am.

I'm about to start rummaging for clues when the door opens, and Tomas pokes his head in again. "We've got clear skies, and Ashford and Finch have finally retired for the evening. You should come topside."

I glance at him. "I'm supposed to be asleep."

He shrugs. "So is everyone, but that doesn't stop Isla from baking at midnight."

I huff a quiet laugh, and he grins like he's proud of himself for getting a chuckle out of me. I stand, still sore, still shaken, but steadier than I was. "Alright, cabin boy. Lead the way."

The deck is quiet, the sea black velvet beneath the moon. A few men move in the shadows, climbing ropes or patrolling slowly with tired eyes.

I step out and let the air hit me, cold, briny, and clean. For the first time since being pulled aboard the ship, I feel the faintest sense of peace.

Tomas perches on a coil of rope and starts picking at a bit of salted fish from a cloth in his pocket. "We're two days from Port Royal. You ever been?"

I laugh. "Not exactly."

He eyes me like he wants to ask more, but he says nothing.

The night is cool and clear, the stars sharp pinpricks against the ink-black sky. The sea laps quietly against the hull of *The Tempest's Vow*, the occasional creak of rigging the only sound besides our breathing.

"Do you ever get used to this? The endless rocking, the smells, the cold that settles in your bones?" I ask.

He shrugs. "No one ever does. You just learn to ignore it—and swear a lot."

I laugh quietly. "I'm still trying not to scream every time I nearly fall over."

From the shadows near the railing, a voice cuts in, dry and calm. "That's the sign of a green deckhand—or a landsman."

I look up to see a lean man stepping into the moonlight, his hands tucked into the pockets of his worn coat. His dark eyes glint with something mischievous.

"Cyrus," Tomas says with a grin. "Our resident wisecracker and tolerable nuisance."

The man gives me a slow, easy smile. "Not so much tolerable as useful. I distract everyone from their misery. It keeps the demons off the crew's backs."

I raise an eyebrow. "How do you distract the crew?"

"By talking too much," Tomas cuts in.

"Precisely." He shrugs. "Either that or telling tales that make the night a little less grim."

Tomas shakes his head but laughs. "He's got a point. Been on more ships than you've had hot meals, and he never met a trouble he couldn't talk his way out of."

I glance at Cyrus, intrigued. "Tell us a tale?"

He leans on the rail, his eyes twinkling. "There once was a great explorer, noble type, boots shined, maps all crisp and folded proper. He found more lands than he could name, a real legend. One night— somewhere off the coast of nowhere—he met a pod of mermaids."

"Mermaids?" Tomas asks.

"A whole shimmerin' school of 'em," Cyrus confirms, wagging a finger. "Long hair, sea-glass eyes, voices like the lullabies of doomed sailors. And they were *smitten* with our brave lad. Told him he was the finest man they'd ever seen. Claimed his nose was chiseled from Poseidon's own statue."

Tomas snorts.

Cyrus grins wider. "Oh, he did more than believe. He *reciprocated*. Said their scales sparkled like the stars and kissed every single one, swearing eternal love. He sang to 'em. Recited poetry. There was weeping. At one point, he composed a sea shanty *on the spot* about their ocean-blue eyes."

Tomas howls. "He was drunk, wasn't he?"

"Oh, positively marinated," Cyrus says. "Come dawn, he wakes up on a sandbar, sun in his face, his mouth tasting like regret, and who's in the water beside him?"

"Let me guess," Tomas says.

"Three sleepy *manatees*," Cyrus declares, spreading his arms like he's just revealed the climax of a grand epic. "Big-eyed, whiskered, wrinkly sea cows, still clinging to him like he's the bloody Neptune of their dreams."

Tomas bursts out laughing. "No!"

"Oh yes," says Cyrus, nodding solemnly. "He wept for days, claiming they were the greatest loves he'd ever known."

Tomas wheezes. "What happened to him?"

"Swore off whiskey, and swore off mermaids," Cyrus says.

We're all laughing now, and Cyrus gives us a mock bow before sauntering off.

The laughter fades, but something warm lingers in its place—a thread of belonging I hadn't expected to find. Tomas stretches out on the deck beside me, his eyes half-closed, and Cyrus hums a tune as he disappears into the shadows. The sea rocks beneath us, steady and endless.

I'm lost in a time I don't understand, haunted by questions I can't answer, but tonight, under a sky full of stars, I feel less alone.

I hope it's enough to keep me afloat.

TEMPEST TEMPTRESS

GABRIEL

The storm breaks just after dawn, the sky bruised gray. Its first pale lights are swallowed by roiling clouds that claw across the horizon—smoke from Neptune's fire. I grip the wheel of the ship with both hands, my boots braced against the slick deck as she bucks beneath me like a beast fighting its leash.

Waves crash over the bow, slamming the hull hard enough to make the timbers groan. Salt and rain blind me, the sting of it slicing across my cheeks, soaking me to the bone. The wind shrieks in my ears, howling through the rigging like a thousand screaming eels, and the sails snap and twist above, struggling not to tear.

"Brace the mainsail!" I bellow over the thunder. "Double reef it—now!"

The crew scrambles like ants in a kicked nest, slipping across the deck, their voices hoarse with effort and fear. Lines are everywhere, tangled, whipping like serpents. The smell of wet rope and oil burns in my nostrils.

A crack of lightning flashes to the east, too close, and in that split-second glare, I scan the deck. I see Finch at the foremast, soaked through and shouting something I can't hear. Two men wrestle with the boom, nearly ripped off their feet. Another stumbles over the rail and only just catches hold.

Where's Sabrina?

I scan again—nothing. Just bodies hunched against the wind, figures blurred by sheets of rain and rolling mist. Panic rises in my chest, hot and sharp, but I crush it down. I can't afford that. Not now.

"Hold her steady!" I shout to the lad at the secondary lines. "Don't let her list!"

A monstrous wave crashes against the starboard side. The deck tilts dangerously, and for a breathless second, I think we'll roll. The wood groans, every board straining, and then she rights herself, slamming back into the swell.

I grit my teeth. "Come on, girl. You've weathered worse than this."

Have we? I'm not sure anymore.

The wind howls again, rising to a pitch that makes my ears ring. The rain is colder now, slanted sideways. I blink hard against it, trying to see beyond the chaos, trying to catch a glimpse of Isla's dark braid or Sabrina's pale skirt, but everything's a blur.

Goddamn it. Where are they?

I think of Isla in the galley, scolding the crew with a ladle in one hand and a blade in the other. I think of her little brother Tomas. If Isla goes over, he'll be alone. And Sabrina—

Her face flashes in my mind. That strange, fierce look in her eyes. Her stubborn grace, and absolute refusal to cower.

Is she below deck? Clinging to something in the dark, praying for it to end? Or has the sea already taken her?

"Captain!" someone shouts near the helm. A man nearly collides with me, one side bloodied, his eyes wild. "Port rig's tearing loose!"

"Cut it free if you have to!" I shout back.

He vanishes into the storm, and the sky flashes again, another bolt, blinding. For a breath, I see the world in silver and shadow, and the wave that follows is taller than the mast.

"Hold fast!" I bellow.

It slams into us, the boat lifting too high, and slams down, the impact shuddering through my spine. Something cracks and groans deep in the belly of the hull. I throw my weight into the wheel, my teeth gritted, my arms burning. She holds, but just barely.

We tilt starboard again, and I hear a man scream, but can't see him, just his shape tumbling down the slick deck, snatched by the sea.

"Damn it all!" I roar. "We're not finished! Stay with her!"

No one answers, but I know they obey. The line holds, the wheel jerks and bucks, but the helm responds. The sails fight the storm, fraying but not yet surrendering. Beneath my soaked coat, my heart hammers.

We're not through it. Not yet, but the boat still sails. My ship still lives. I grip the wheel tighter and fix my eyes on the distant light to the west—a patch of calm that hasn't yet been swallowed. We'll reach it. We have to.

"Hold steady!" I shout again, hoarse now. "She's not going down today!" Not while I still stand. Not while I still draw breath.

The storm is a living beast, and tonight, it means to devour us. Waves tower like cathedral walls, slamming down against *The Vow* with enough force to shake the bones of every man aboard. The rain is relentless—cold knives against my skin. Lightning shreds the sky, and thunder answers like cannon fire, drowning even the sound of men screaming.

I cling to the wheel, soaked to the marrow, my jaw clenched so tight it aches. The ship bucks again, her bow rising nearly vertical before crashing down into a trough. Water floods across the deck.

"Reef the foresail!" I roar, voice tearing from my throat. "Get her nose into the wind!"

Boots thud on the planks, shouts blend with the storm, but it's not enough. The rigging groans overhead like it might snap. Every rope is a whip, lashing. Every sail is a shroud waiting to fall.

And then I hear it. A thin, terrified cry.

"Help!"

I snap my head toward the sound. Through sheets of rain, I spot a small figure clinging to the rail near the mainmast, half-submerged as the next wave crashes over.

Tomas. Bloody hell.

He's too light, too small to be up here in this storm. His hands are slipping, his face white with panic. I shove the wheel into the hands of a nearby sailor.

"Keep her steady!" I bark, already sprinting across the deck.

The wind knocks me sideways. I grab a rope, anchor myself, and charge forward. Water slaps my legs. Lightning flashes again, and I see Tomas losing his grip.

"Don't you let go!" I bellow.

His eyes find mine. He's shaking, utterly terrified. His fingers slip.

I lunge the last few steps, slam my knee into the railing, and catch him just as his grip gives out. His entire weight slams into me. I hook my arm around his chest and haul him back from the edge.

"You trying to get yourself killed, lad?" I shout, yanking him upright.

"I was looking for Isla!" he chokes. "She wasn't below. I thought she came topside—"

"You bloody fool!" I snap. But the anger dies as fast as it arrives. He's drenched, trembling, coughing water. He's just a lad. A brave, reckless lad.

"Below deck. Now," I order him, dragging him toward the companionway. Another wave crashes over us, nearly knocking us down. Tomas coughs, but keeps pace. We're almost to the hatch when the sky splits in two.

I look up just in time to see a loose boom swinging wildly— untethered in the wind.

"Down!" I shout, shoving Tomas to the planks.

The boom whistles past, missing us by inches, and slams into the deck with a thunderous crack. Splinters fly, and a man screams.

"Tomas, go!" I shove him toward the hatch. "Find shelter, and don't come back up."

He hesitates, soaked curls plastered to his face. "But Isla—"

"I'll find her."

He stares at me, then nods once and vanishes below.

I turn back to the chaos. The crew's falling apart, men too scared or soaked to move right, others barely holding the lines. Above it all, the storm keeps howling, louder than anyone can pray.

"Get the mainsheet down!" I shout. "Cut it free if you have to!"

Lightning cracks again, illuminating the deck in stark white. I see three men wrestling with a torn sail, as another slips and vanishes over the rail.

I bite down a curse. Where the hell is Isla? Where's Sabrina?

A knot of dread coils tighter in my gut. I should've kept them all locked below. I should've—

No time for regrets. I grab a rope and scale the quarterdeck again. My hands are raw, bleeding, and my coat's heavy with seawater. The wheel bucks as I take it back, the helm screaming under my grip.

We ride another wave, one, two, three heartbeats in the air, then crash down again. *The Vow* moans, and I can feel her bones splintering beneath me. She's tired, but she's not done.

"Come on, ol' lass," I growl. "Not today."

Behind me, the sails flap in jagged rhythm, and the wind bellows with the voice of Neptune. I will not let this ship go down. Not while my crew still breathes, and not while I still have strength in my body to fight.

I plant myself, square my shoulders, and grip the wheel harder. The storm can take its best shot, but I'm not letting go.

The wind doesn't die all at once. It pulls back in fits, a wounded beast still lashing out, refusing to admit it's lost its grip. The waves don't vanish, but they shrink until the deck's rhythm becomes something almost safe. Not familiar, not steady, but no longer deadly.

I ease my hands off the wheel slightly. They're raw, blistered, blood trickling, and my right shoulder aches with the strain. My legs feel like they might collapse beneath me.

A glance at the sails tells me what I need to know—two torn, one half-loose, but still enough cloth to keep us moving. The rigging's a mess, and I'll need every man sober and mending by nightfall to reset it, if the wind holds steady.

Thunder rumbles in the distance, fading now, Mother Nature's grudge she hasn't quite let go. The clouds above thin to a dull slate gray, heavy with leftover rain, but no longer bleeding fury. The worst of it has passed.

I turn in time to see Elias heading down the ladder, his hair plastered to his forehead and coat soaked through. He moves quickly, without a word, his eyes locked on the hatch.

"Where are you going?" I call after him.

He doesn't break stride. "Below."

"For what?"

"To check on things."

That's all he says. Then he's gone, disappearing into the shadows below deck like a man hunting something, or someone. I stare after him, frowning.

A crewman lurches toward me—Darwin, a steady hand. "We've secured the mainsail, Cap'n. Took a beating, but she'll hold."

"Good," I say. "Tell Briggs to clear the deck. I want the wounded accounted for. Dead, too."

He nods grimly and vanishes down the ladder. I exhale slowly. The storm's passed, but the damage is just beginning to show, and I still don't know where Sabrina is.

The name catches in my mind like a splinter. She's not my problem. A stowaway, a castaway, a ghost from nowhere. We'll drop her at Port Royal, same as planned. She'll vanish into the city's chaos, and we'll sail on without her. That's the plan, but that doesn't stop me from scanning the ruined deck again. She's not among the figures in the hauling line. Not near the mainmast. She's not huddled by the rail, not moving cargo or tending to the wounded. Which means—

She might be below deck, or she might've gone overboard. Either way, it's not my concern. I don't care.

I curse under my breath and turn the wheel over to the boatswain.

"I'll be back," I mutter.

The ladder is slick with seawater, and some of the lanterns below deck are still lit in the narrow corridor as I pass. I make for the lower berths, moving past hammocks and crates.

When I hear Elias's voice, low and firm, I slow down. It's muffled enough to make the words indistinct, but I can hear the tone. Not angry or cruel, just focused.

I round the corner just in time to catch sight of his back. He's crouched beside Sabrina, wrapped in a blanket. She's sitting on a cot, soaked through but upright. Her hair is tangled, her face pale, but her eyes meet mine.

Elias glances back at me, his jaw tight. "She's not dead," he says flatly.

And neither is Isla, who I spot across the small room, cradling a bruised arm and murmuring something to her brother, who clutches her like he'll never let go again.

I step inside, water dripping from my coat. My heart still hammers, slow and angry, in my chest.

"I thought you went overboard," I say to Sabrina.

She lifts her chin, the blanket slipping from her shoulders. "I was below, where I was told to stay."

"I couldn't find you," I say, voice rougher than I intend.

"I didn't know I was supposed to be in the habit of reporting to you."

"You're on my ship," I snap. "You're my responsibility until you step off."

I shift my weight, glancing around the dim, dripping berth. Isla's speaking softly to Tomas in the corner. Elias hovers by the hatch, pretending not to listen. My eyes fall back to Sabrina.

"You should rest," I say. "There'll be work to do once the sun comes back out."

She shoots me a hard look, her eyes still burning with that stubborn fire. "Rest, huh? Since when do you give a damn if I'm rested or not?"

I smirk. "Since I'd rather have you working on my deck than floating in the water feeding the fish."

Her lip curls, half sneer, half smile. "You're not the bloody tyrant you think you are, Captain."

I step closer, close enough that she can see the challenge in my eyes. "But I *am* the one who keeps this ship from sinking, and I'm the one who protects you."

She meets my stare, unflinching. "Don't get soft on me, Captain."

"Soft's the last thing you'll ever get from me."

Sabrina's cheeks flush, and she lets the blanket slip just enough to reveal a hint of skin before she leans in, voice low. "Good. I like a challenge worth gripping onto."

Her brazen boldness catches me off guard, stirring something deep and wild I didn't expect, and I hate how much it thrills me.

"Wouldn't expect anything less." I glance toward the hatch, stepping back before this charge between us ignites like lightning in a bottle.

I climb back up onto the top deck. The sky is clearing, but my thoughts stay tangled in her—alluring, stubborn, fierce, humorous, and impossible to forget.

The Tempest's Vow moans beneath my boots, but it's the fire sparking between Sabrina and me that pulls my thoughts back to her.

FIRE AND RAIN

Sabrina

The storm is a roaring lion above, shaking the ship's bones and rattling the lanterns, threatening to shatter. I clutch the damp wood of the bulkhead, trying to steady myself as *The Tempest's Vow* pitches and rolls beneath me. The wind screams, tearing at the rigging above. Rain thrashes the deck, and somewhere, a line snaps—a sharp crack like a gunshot that sets my heart racing.

"Stay below deck!" Elias's order rings in my ears, but staying still feels impossible. I'm pinned by the chaos, and by fear.

Retreating to the berth where Isla and I sleep, the cramped space barely sheltering me from the cold, the cot slides with every crash of the ship. The smell of salt and sweat clings to the walls. I huddle beneath a threadbare blanket.

I imagine Gabriel with his smoky gaze, and the way he commands the ship like a god of the sea himself.

But the questions I haven't yet fully explored are, *Where exactly am I? What year is it? What nightmare have I fallen into?*

Those thoughts claw at me until I can't bear it. I slip quietly out of the berth, careful not to get caught.

The corridors are narrow and slick, the wood groaning under the strain of the sky's assault. I've glimpsed the captain's study before. It stands slightly ajar, as if waiting for me. I push it open and slip inside, the scent of leather and ink wrapping around me like a shroud.

The room is small but cramped with papers, ledgers, and maps pinned haphazardly to the walls. The desk is cluttered with quills, inkpots, a battered compass. I scan the pages scattered there, my heart pounding with a mixture of dread and hope.

I find a thick, leather-bound journal and pry it open, the pages murky but legible. I flip through it fast, names and dates blurring together until—there it is.

May 1692.

I feel like I've been punched in the gut. The year hangs in the air, cold and cruel.

1692. Port Royal.

The city I love. The city I've studied—the jewel of the Caribbean, bustling and decadent. The city that *will* be swallowed by the Earth in a monstrous earthquake, that *will* sink beneath the sea in hours, drowning thousands.

I close the journal with a snap. My chest tightens, a sudden panic twisting deep in my stomach. The wrath of the heavens outside isn't just some passing fury—it's a warning.

I stumble back, pressing my palms against the desk to steady myself. The ship creaks and groans, but suddenly, it all feels even more fragile, as if the entire world could shatter with the next wave.

I pace the cramped room, my mind racing. The knowledge burns like fire, filling me with a desperate urgency I can't shake.

I freeze, my breath caught in my throat as footsteps thunder closer. The door creaks—no, it's not the captain or Elias—too slow, too considerate.

"Isla?" I whisper, barely daring to hope.

The door opens wider, and there she is—her dark hair plastered to her forehead, her eyes filled with worry and cheeks flushed from the wind. "Sabrina, what are you doing here?" Her voice is low, urgent, but there's no anger.

She moves closer, glancing nervously over her shoulder, then lays a steadying hand on my arm. "We have to get out of here. We are forbidden from the captain's quarters."

Isla's hand tightens on my arm, strength in her grip. "Sabrina, you have to come back. Now. The raging fury's tearing the ship apart out there. It's no time for us to be wandering around, especially here."

I swallow hard, the weight of her words pressing on my chest. The cabin feels impossibly small, the walls closing in with every thunderclap shaking the ship.

"We don't know where Tomas is," Isla says, her voice trembling. "He could be anywhere, and if the captain or Elias finds you here… you'll be in more trouble than this howler can bring."

Her dark eyes search mine, pleading. "We need to go where it's safer. Come on. Before it gets worse."

I hesitate, torn between the desperate urge to keep looking for answers and the cold truth. Isla doesn't wait for me to decide. She grabs my hand, pulling me toward the door. The floorboards shudder beneath us as the ship lurches violently.

"Keep low," Isla warns as we move through the hallways, her voice difficult to hear. "And don't make a sound."

The roar of the deluge outside is a constant threat, but inside, the fear of getting caught feels sharper than any wave.

We reach the cramped berth, and she pushes the door open, the tiny, familiar space offering a thin shield. Isla exhales shakily, pulls me inside, and prays aloud for her brother.

A few moments later, the door rattles open, and Tomas stumbles in, coughing and shivering, water dripping from his sleeves and boots.

"Oh, thank heavens," Isla says breathlessly, hugging her brother.

She lets go, and Tomas sinks onto the edge of the cot, shaking so hard I'm afraid he'll shatter. His teeth chatter, and his hands tremble as he pulls his soaked jacket tighter around his thin frame.

The storm still screams outside, the ship creaking and groaning beneath the relentless assault. Every thunderclap sends a fresh wave of panic through me, a primal fear that claws at my throat. I force myself to breathe, to stay present.

Isla's voice softens. "You should sit down, Sabrina. The storm's not letting up anytime soon."

I nod, but my mind races. The journal's date—1692—loops in my head like a curse. I can't say a word. If I reveal that I know what's coming, what *will* come, it could change everything. Or worse, get me branded a witch or a liar.

"I—" I start, then stop. The weight of my secret presses down, suffocating.

Tomas looks up at me, his eyes filled with awe. "You didn't go overboard this time," he says quietly, as if that's already a miracle.

The ship shudders violently, and the lanterns threaten to blow, casting the room in shifting shadows. The storm outside is a wild beast, and I feel utterly powerless before it.

Isla moves closer, kneeling beside me. "We'll be fine. I've seen storms worse than this," she says, voice gentle.

I force a small nod. The wind howls again, rattling the small windowpane. I close my eyes briefly, wishing for calm and safety.

Tomas curls up on Isla's cot, still trembling, his damp curls plastered to his forehead. Isla sits beside me, her knees pulled up tight to her chest, her arm pressed against mine for warmth.

I lean my back against the wall, listening to the ship groan. Every pitch and shudder makes my stomach twist. A gust of wind screams through the upper decks, and something heavy crashes above us. Then a monstrous wave hits us broadside.

The Vow tilts too hard, and all at once, we're weightless.

We're thrown across the berth, slammed into the opposite wall— the one with the door. My shoulder hits first, and the breath is knocked from my lungs. Isla crashes beside me with a cry. Tomas hits the floor with a grunt, his arms flailing.

The porthole creaks, then snaps open under the pressure—and water bursts in. Not a flood, not yet—but enough to slosh in, and soak us in a freezing splash.

"Out," Isla gasps, scrambling to her knees. "We have to get out."

I don't argue. I reach for Tomas, who's still dazed, and we crawl, wet, sore and shaking, into the corridor. The floor is slick beneath us.

Saltwater puddles in the cracks. My body shivers uncontrollably as I lean against the opposite wall, pulling Tomas into the shelter of my arm. Isla sits close beside us, silent, her face pale with worry.

For what feels like hours, we just sit there. Above, the onslaught still screams, but not quite as loud. The worst may be passing. Or maybe I've just gone numb.

The wind starts to shift, losing its edge. The ship still rocks, but not as violently. Thunder sounds further off now, more like a memory than a threat. We sit together, huddled and soaked, our hearts still pounding.

Then footsteps echo on the ladder above. A moment later, Elias appears at the top of the hallway, soaked through, his eyes scanning us fast and sharp.

"There you are," he says, his voice tight. "Come on. Let's get you dried off before you catch your death."

Elias doesn't wait for us to move. He strides past, heading down the hall with a purposeful pace, then circles back to herd us forward like wayward ducks.

I follow, dazed, still shivering. My mind is a tangle of fear and disbelief about the weather, about the year, about everything, and none of it makes sense right now. I'm too tired, and too cold.

Instead of leading us above deck, Elias veers back into the berth, the one I crawled out of. He strikes flint to the small hearth in the wall, coaxing flame from the damp tinder like he's done it a hundred times. The warmth is immediate, even if it's faint. I crouch beside Isla and Tomas as Elias moves around us, setting the cots upright with brisk, efficient hands.

Then, from a shelf built into the corner, Elias pulls down three folded blankets made of thick wool, dry and warm. He tosses one to Tomas, drapes the next over Isla's shoulders, and holds the last one out to me.

Why is he being kind now, of all times? Elias has made it clear I'm nothing more than a burden, but now he's building fires, fixing cots, handing out dry blankets like some reluctant guardian. Maybe it's the first mate's duty, or maybe he cares for Isla and Tomas.

The door creaks open, and Gabriel steps in, drenched, scowling, eyes sweeping the berth like he's ready to tear it apart. His gaze lands on me, and something sharp glows behind his eyes: relief, maybe, or fury, or both, but all I can think is that he's alive. He's alive. He's soaked to the bone with that wild look in his eyes.

And he's never looked more maddeningly, infuriatingly handsome.

* * *

The torrential rains are long gone, but their aftermath lingers in every soaked plank and frayed rope of the ship. The scent of salt and smoke clings to the air, mingling with the smell of fish stew simmering in the pot over the small galley fire. I slice vegetables beside Isla while Tomas peels what might be yams—though he keeps sneaking bites when he thinks we're not looking.

Outside, the crew works, climbing the rigging, mending sails, clearing the deck, hammering splintered beams back into place. Every so often, someone lets out a bark of laughter or a groan of pain. *The Tempest's Vow* survived, but only barely.

Isla stirs the pot, Tomas hums a tune under his breath, and I can't stop thinking.

Not about the storm or even about the city we're sailing toward—though the thought of Port Royal, knowing what's coming, makes a pit open in my stomach every time I let myself linger there.

No. My mind's still trapped back in that cabin, locked in the heat of Gabriel Ashford's gaze.

Soft. Hard. Gripping. I can't believe I let my full New York City personality blast through like that—*in a British accent*, no less—on a ship sailing through the Caribbean in 1692, with some pirate captain who I can't even tell if he wants to toss me overboard or toss me into his bed.

I drop a piece of carrot into the stew a little harder than necessary, scowling at myself. What was I even trying to say? Why didn't I just shut up and let the moment pass?

Because it *was* a moment, there's no denying that. That heat wasn't all from the fire Elias started. I felt it. I know Gabriel did too.

I rub my forehead and mutter a curse. It's not like I wanted to flirt with some pirate captain from the seventeenth century.

"Careful," Isla says gently, nodding toward my fingers. "You nearly took the tip of that one off."

I realize I've been gripping the knife too tight.

Gripping. Great. Now I'm thinking about that again.

I shake my head, trying to focus. "Sorry. Still a bit shaken."

Isla gives me a knowing glance. Tomas drops a chunk of yam into the pot with a splash and grins.

I glance out the open hatch. Gabriel's on deck somewhere. That look he gave me like I'd shocked him, like I'd tempted him, burned itself into my brain. I didn't mean to light a fire in him, but hell, part of me is glad I did, and that's almost as terrifyingly exciting as what's waiting for me in Port Royal.

The door swings open, and the room shifts with it not because of the breeze, but because *he* walks in.

Somehow, Gabriel is already clean, dry, and maddeningly composed. His fresh dry shirt is undone, his sleeves rolled to the elbows, his chest annoyingly broad and very much in my line of sight.

He surveys the galley. "Smells edible," he says, glancing into the stew pot like it might bite him. His eyes move to mine. "And you haven't burned the ship down. I'm impressed."

"I considered it," I say. "But after what she just endured, I assumed she's invincible."

He laughs, takes the bowl, sits across from me, and eats like a man who hasn't had a hot meal in a week. When his gaze lifts to mine, slow, and so sharp it should come with a warning label, there's heat there. The kind that curls low and makes me forget every single reason flirting with a pirate is a bad idea.

"Is that so?" he says finally, his voice smooth. "And what kind of motivation would you have to burn her down?" The question is playful.

"Well, could be that I'm sick of sailing. Could be that the Captain of the ship is a savage lord of the sea," I say with a wink.

Gabriel leans back, his eyes glittering with amusement. "And here I thought you were the fiercest tempest I've ever had to weather."

I smirk, tilting my head. "Careful, Captain. Keep calling me a tempest, and I might just show you exactly how wet and wild things can get."

He chuckles. "You are not only a temptress, but a mischievous little minx as well."

Captain Ashford finishes the last bite, sets his bowl down with a soft clink, rises, and confidently strides toward the door.

He stops just before stepping out and looks back at me, that crooked grin still playing at his lips. "Don't go threatening to set the ship on fire again, Sabrina. I might just have to make you walk the plank."

Then he's gone down the hall, leaving a charged silence in his wake.

Isla leans close, a sly smile tugging at her lips. "Well, if that's not enough to keep your heart racing, I don't know what is."

I shoot her a sharp look, my cheeks heating up, but hell if I'm not secretly grateful for the spark he's lit inside me.

SECRETS AND SPARKS

The storm has passed, leaving the sea groaning and stretching beneath us, and above deck, the crew moves with that particular mix of fatigue and relief known only to sailors who've seen death leering from the waves and survived to mock it. Men mutter, lines are re-coiled, sails patched, bruises checked, and laughter rises again in the spaces between orders.

And I've been distracted, thinking of Sabrina. My gaze keeps drifting back to her. She moves with an ease that portrays either confidence or recklessness; I haven't decided which. She's no longer the stranger cowering in borrowed clothes, but neither is she someone I've figured out entirely, and it's the not-knowing that puts my instincts on edge. Still, there's something about the way she matches me wit for wit, how she never quite defers or flatters. She lets her silences stretch without filling them with small pleasantries.

Yes, I'm drawn to her gorgeous eyes and striking features, but what keeps me awake at night, what gnaws at the edge of my thoughts when I should be sleeping, is the way Sabrina moves through this world without apology. That kind of freedom is not common among women. It's dangerous, absolutely maddening, and I can't look away.

So tonight, when the wind has gone quiet and the lanterns flicker with a tired, amber glow, I send for her.

Sabrina arrives at my cabin door. "You summoned me," she says, not quite amused, not quite bothered.

"I did," I reply, already reaching for the rum. "Please, sit."

My quarters are cramped, cluttered with maps and charts, and the smell of tobacco smoke clings to everything. I pour two modest glasses and slide one across the table toward her.

She takes the chair across from mine and looks at the drink before lifting it with a raised brow. "Is this your way of interrogating me or seducing me? I find I can never quite tell with you."

"Who says I can't do both?"

She grins. "Oh, so it'll be like every other first date I've ever been on."

The phrase "date" used in this manner confuses me and piques my curiosity. I lean forward in my chair. "First date?" I ask, testing the waters.

"Or—courtship. Uh… what did you call me into your study to discuss?" she replies, flustered, stumbling slightly as she speaks, and for just a moment, her accent slips.

The posh English tone she usually wears like armor falls away, and something sharper breaks through: quicker, rougher, the kind of voice you'd expect from a brawler in a tavern, not a lady on deck. It's gone in an instant, tucked back into place, but I caught it.

She's not the type to shrink from attention. Hell, she's bolder than most men I've met. She voices her opinions like cannon fire and flirts back like it's a duel she intends to win. Nor does she soften herself for anyone. She doesn't care if the crew curses or shouts something bawdy when she passes, and that kind of defiance, I'll admit, has grown on me. There's something exhilarating about a woman who refuses to be small.

Alas, her accent, and the way that she occasionally uses strange words and phrases, doesn't make sense. It doesn't suit the rest of her, the woman who glares down seasoned sailors and laughs when I threaten to throw her overboard.

Why someone like her would pretend to be someone else bothers me more than I want to admit. I swirl the rum in my glass, leaning back just enough to study her properly. She's watching me, too, waiting to see if I'll comment on the slip.

I won't yet. Although, it's one more piece of her, and damn if I don't want to figure her out.

"Why did I call you here?" I ask, my voice low, my eyes fixed on hers. "The storm's passed, the ship's quieter, and some things are better said in the calm. You held your own out there, and I don't say that to just anyone."

The second glass of rum burns less than the first. Across the table, Sabrina's cheeks have flushed slightly, and she's lounging in my chair like she owns the place, her boot tucked under her, her fingers toying with the rim of her glass.

"Tell me the truth," she says, tipping her head to the side. "Do you always invite suspicious women into your cabin for drinks, or am I just fortunate?"

I smirk. "I don't know how fortunate you are," I say, letting the words linger, "but you're definitely special."

She raises a brow, pretending to scoff, but there's a smile tugging at the corner of her mouth. "Careful, Captain. That almost sounded sincere."

"Almost. Though I never said whether you were special in a good way… or a cursed one."

Sabrina laughs. "Tell me, what were you like before all this?" she asks.

"All what?"

"This," she says, gesturing around lazily. "Captain. Pirate. Brooding sea god."

I huff a laugh. "Younger," I say. "Not nearly as wise."

She grins. "Do go on."

"I was the second son. Didn't matter what I did, I was never going to be the heir, never going to inherit anything but trouble. So I left, or tried to. I joined up under a man I respected."

Her expression softens a touch. "A captain?"

I nod. "My brother, James."

There it is, his name, out before I think to guard it. She doesn't interrupt, just shifts forward slightly in her chair. Her presence is completely disarming and beautiful.

"James was everything I wasn't," I say, my voice quieter now. "Level-headed. Thoughtful. He made people want to follow him, not because he barked orders, but because he carried himself like nothing could shake him. My brother wasn't the sort to chase glory or make a show of courage. He had a quiet strength that anchored those around him. When chaos erupted, he didn't panic or lose his head. Instead, he faced it with a calm that made you believe we might just get through it."

"You speak of your brother in the past tense," she says, quieter now. "Did something happen to him?"

"Spanish ship," I say. "We'd split our crews—James took the lead vessel, and I was on the other, a day behind. Should've been routine, but they came out of nowhere, hitting him hard and fast. By the time we caught up, it was too late. The ship was still burning, and there were no survivors, just wreckage and ash. He died before I could get to him, and I've had to live with the fact that I wasn't there."

She's quiet, watching me, but she doesn't interrupt.

"I don't talk about him much," I say. "But there's not a day I don't think about that damned delay. About what I might've done if I'd reached him in time."

Sabrina doesn't speak right away but then softly whispers, "I'm sorry."

I nod once, not trusting my voice. I've had time to bury that day beneath command and routine, but grief doesn't rot away. It just settles deeper, like water in the hull.

"He sounds like someone worth remembering."

"He was," I say, my voice low. "Best man I've ever known."

A moment passes, then with that maddening tilt of her head and a slight curve at the edge of her mouth, she says, "Explains a few things."

I narrow my eyes. "Such as?"

She shrugs, feigning innocence. "The way you scowl when something doesn't go well. The brooding is classic younger sibling energy."

I chuckle. "Younger by two years, although he never let me forget it."

She raises her glass. "To James, and to the brother who'd still deck a man for him."

I tap mine to hers, the clink soft in the quiet room. "To James."

We drink, and something shifts in the air again a touch, the way it always does with her. One minute it's serious, the next it's flirtatious, and I never know which way she'll spin it.

"You know," she says, tilting her head, "if you ever tire of captaining this whole misfit navy of yours, I imagine you'd make an excellent tavern tender. Smoldering stares, tragic backstory, hands built for trouble…. You're very marketable."

My lips twitch. "You trying to recruit me, Sabrina?"

She shrugs, her eyes dancing. "I've recruited worse."

"I'm not easy to employ," I warn her.

She leans forward, her eyes sharp, like she's daring me. "Would you ever let a woman be in charge of you?"

I hold her gaze, slowly and deliberately. "Only if she knows how to make a man want to follow."

Her laugh is low and rough. "And what would she have to do to earn that?"

"Make it clear she's the one holding the whip, and that surrender isn't weakness."

She bites her lip, her eyes darkening with challenge. "Surrender could be bliss."

"A man who doesn't know that, doesn't know what he's missing."

Candlelight catches her soft curves, an unspoken reminder that beneath all her sharpness, she's still very much a soft woman.

Something's building between us, and it's enough to be dangerous. It hums beneath the surface of every word we trade, tightening low in my gut, daring me to move closer. I didn't expect this. I didn't think I'd open up to her the way I have tonight. Hell, I was meant to be questioning *her*, peeling back whatever lies she'd spun to get on my ship, but somewhere after the third drink, I forgot. Sabrina makes it too natural and uncomplicated to share with her.

For a moment, I wonder what would happen if I crossed the space between us, but before I can act on my lust, she draws a slow breath and stands.

"I should go," she says, not quite meeting my eye. "I'm tired."

She's not lying, but it's not exhaustion that's sending her out that door. It's the same thing holding me in my chair; the fire, the edge. That instinct that if we keep talking, we won't stop at words.

I rise with her. "What'll you do in Port Royal," I ask, "if you don't find the people in your party?"

She turns back to me with a mischievous smile, something wicked behind her eyes. "Haven't quite figured out where I'll stay or what I'll do yet."

Sabrina's hand rests briefly on the doorframe, then she adds, with a tilt of her head and a spark that could burn the sails off this ship: "But I do know the first thing I'll buy is a whip," she says coyly, and she slips out without another word.

The door clicks shut, and I'm stunned, caught off guard by just how quickly and thoroughly she's gotten under my skin. Beautiful, clever, bold—and damn it, she knows exactly what to say to drive me mad.

DRESSING THE PORT

Sabrina

My mind keeps drifting back to last night in Gabriel's study. The low flicker of candlelight, the warmth of the rum, the way we spoke to each other with flirtatious banter. The drinks and heat–I just can't shake it.

I shouldn't let it mean anything, but the conversation came too easily, and that kind of ease is dangerous, especially with a man like Gabriel. He was built for storms, chaos, and hard decisions. He moves through the world like nothing can touch him. Men like that don't slow down for anyone, and I can't afford to get attached.

How can I become part of Gabriel's life when I don't even belong in this century? I have no idea where I'll sleep tonight, or how long I can keep pretending I'm part of this world.

I grip the rail of the ship as the breeze kicks up, strands of my hair whipping across my cheeks. The sea has settled into a gray-blue stretch that reaches endlessly toward the horizon, and it's stunning, but the knot in my stomach only tightens. Port Royal is close now, and Gabriel will have no use for me once we dock. I'm not a sailor, not crew, and soon he'll sail off toward whatever trouble waits for him next, and I'll be stuck in a century that doesn't know what to do with a woman who talks back.

I miss home; I miss Maddie, and for the first time since all this began, it actually occurs to me: Maddie could be here! It's probably wishful thinking, but maybe she got tossed into the same storm and the same century. Maybe when we dock, I'll see her standing in the crowd, just as confused and out of place as I am. The thought hits me out of nowhere, sharp and sudden, and I can't believe I haven't let myself consider it until now. It's a long shot, sure, but so was everything else that's happened, and if there's even a chance she's in Port Royal, I have to find her.

"Land ho!"

The cry cuts across the deck, and my heart jumps.

All around me, the crew scrambles into motion. Above, the sails snap. Below, ropes are coiled and orders barked. We've arrived at Port Royal.

I catch sight of Gabriel at the helm, shouting something over the wind, all command and motion, his coat billowing behind him like something out of a film. He doesn't look at me. Of course he doesn't. He's got more important things on his mind.

I square my shoulders and head below deck. Isla finds me first. She's smiling, flour still dusting her arms from the morning bread. Tomas is close behind her.

"I guess this is goodbye," I say, trying for lightness. "Thank you, both of you, for everything. Your friendship means so much to me."

"Now, don't forget about us, and you'll be all right," Isla says, pulling me into a tight hug. "Just keep that sharp tongue of yours in check long enough to get a roof over your head."

Tomas salutes with two fingers. "If you need backup robbing a tavern or charming a governor, send word."

I laugh. "Deal."

* * *

The streets of Port Royal unfold before me like a dream—only louder, brighter, more alive than I ever imagined. It's everything I used to study in textbooks and documentaries: the infamous pirate haven, the crown jewel of the Caribbean, the city that was too wild to last. Sunlight gleams off rooftops and gold-toothed grins, while children dash between carts stacked high with tropical fruit and cages of squawking birds. Music floats out from taverns even though it's barely midday. My heart pounds. I can't believe I'm actually here.

This is the city I obsessed over in college, the place I daydreamed about walking through, camera in hand, notebook at the ready. Only now there are no cameras, no travel guides, and no safe return ticket.

I scan every face as I move through the crowded street, my eyes darting from one stranger to the next, hoping I'll spot Maddie. It's hard to vanish into the noise when everything around me feels like it was pulled from the pages of a book and dropped, blazing and alive, into terrifying reality. It's overwhelming, electric, and everything I'd hoped for, just not like this. Not without her.

A bell chimes as I duck into a narrow little shop tucked between a blacksmith and a bakery. The air inside is cooler, shaded. It smells of soap and clean linen. The shop is cramped but rich with color: bolts of fabric, lace, gowns hung like trophies along the walls.

"Help you?" a woman asks from somewhere behind a curtain. She steps into view, gray-haired and small.

I manage a nod. "I need something to wear. Something more...."

She lifts her hand in a silent gesture of understanding and beckons me to follow her to a partition. There, she hands me a few garments, her French accent gentle and motherly. "Take your time, belle," she says with a warm smile. "You've got the natural form for all of these gowns. My name is Odette. Shout if you need me."

I slip behind the curtain and find myself surrounded by silks, satins, and cottons in shades of rose, cream, midnight blue, and pale green. The dresses are trimmed in lace and tiny bows, with sleeves that puff and gather at the elbow. Corsets embroidered with pearls and soft floral patterns. It's like stepping into a painting, or more accurately, a museum display come to life. These are the kinds of gowns I've only seen behind glass, preserved and faded with time. I touch the fabric like it might dissolve in my hands.

The corset takes a while. Boning digs into my ribs as I twist to fasten it, and my fingers are clumsy with the ties. The laces fight back, and I silently curse whoever thought this was an acceptable daily routine, but when I finally get it on, my breath shallow and arms aching, I pull the dress over my head and smooth the delicate skirts into place.

The rose with pearl detailing at the bodice and ribbons at the sleeves is the most delicate thing I've ever worn, and somehow, it fits like it was made for me. I turn slowly, letting the skirt swish with the movement. The fabric catches the light from the small window, and for a moment, I forget where, *when*, and even *who* I am.

When I face the mirror, I actually flinch. Not because I look bad, but because I look like someone else. Perhaps someone who belongs here, like I'm catching a glimpse of a version of me from another life.

I want every gown in the shop. I want to try them all. The silks and satins, the linen day dresses and scandalous evening gowns. I want to be every version of the woman in the mirror, even if for only a moment.

I try on a few more. The fabric brushes like water over my skin as I step into pale green with tiny silver buttons and gauzy sleeves that shimmer when I move. It's exquisite, all of them are, and I'm knee deep in silk, lace, and fantasies I can't afford. And that's the problem.

I stare at the pile of garments draped over the back of the chair. The first few were for fun, curiosity, but now, I've tried on six. Maybe seven. I've been in this shop too long, and I've bought exactly nothing.

Odette was being polite, but I've worked retail. If I don't buy something soon, she might think I'm stealing.

And maybe I should, maybe I have to steal just one dress. It's not like I have any other options. I have no purse, no currency, and no gold coins.

The gown on the hanger, one I haven't tried on yet, is a rich midnight blue with a delicately embroidered bodice in silver threads of scattered stars. I don't belong in this century, but maybe if I dress like I do, no one will question me. I could blend in. I could survive....

I try on the blue one and stare at the gown in the mirror, still half-laced, my hands hovering near the bodice like touching it too long will make it disappear. When I finish with the laces, it fits better than anything I've worn since landing in this century, and for the first time in days, I don't feel like I just crawled out of a ship's cargo hold. But the sensation crawling up my spine isn't comfort. It's panic. Isla's old clothes sit in a crumpled heap beside the chair, torn, gritty, and stretched out in all the wrong places.

Walking out in this dress is theft, and yet if I want to have even a shot at surviving here, I have to look like I belong. I could probably find a place to sleep and something to eat more easily if I am alluring tonight, and that's why this decision is so heavy, like I'm trading one kind of danger for another. I'll figure out how to pay for it later, if I make it through the week.

I hear the bell chime, then boots thudding from the front of the store, and my heart leaps. I peek around the partition and freeze, caught between panic and disbelief.

Oh no, she really does think I'm stealing, and she called on the naval officers.

My mind races, and I realize with growing terror that I am still wearing a dress I have no money to pay for. The rose gown slips off the chair and puddles on the floor. I snatch it up, my hands trembling, and slide slowly back behind the changing curtain, barely daring to breathe.

They're not looking for me. I try to believe it. I repeat it like a prayer. *She had no time to signal them, and they're not looking for me.*

What happens when they ask for my name? Or when I can't produce a single coin, paper or explanation? What happens when they realize I have no people, no home, no identity—just a body in stolen clothes, in the wrong time?

My breath stutters. I press myself flat against the wall, the curtain between me and their world too thin to be comforting. I shut my eyes and try to slow the hammering in my chest.

One voice, rough and impatient, says, "Is this the place? We're lookin' for a man—Jenkins. Been seen near here?"

A softer, but firmer, voice answers, "No, sir. I haven't seen anyone by that name. You're mistaken if you think he's been here."

I recognize the old woman's voice. Odette, the shopkeeper.

"We've had reports. Can't be too careful," an officer says.

Odette's tone remains polite but unyielding. "I'm afraid no one like that comes here. Just ladies lookin' for finery, and gentlemen looking for tailored coats."

After a moment, the footsteps shift, heavy boots moving away from the counter. "Very well," the deep voice mutters. "We'll check elsewhere."

The door closes behind them, and the shop returns to its quiet stillness. My body slowly uncoils as relief floods through me. *They're not after me—not this time.*

I step out from behind the curtain, my heart hammering like a drum. Just as I catch my breath, I see movement through the shop's front window.

Oh, hell no. It's him. Gabriel.

He's walking up the street with that effortless stride. He seems so sure, so commanding, and damn, he is handsome. Goosebumps prickle my skin.

I'm still wearing the dark blue dress, and the way it hugs me, I know I look good. That's not the problem. The problem is I still can't pay for the dress I'm wearing, paired with the wild, ridiculous timing: just when I'm catching my breath after nearly losing it over the cops, here he is.

My throat tightens as Gabriel steps into the shop with that calm confidence he wears, his eyes immediately locking on me. For a split second, something shifts in him, a subtle tightening of his jaw, a slow intake of breath, like he's caught off guard by how much the sight of me pulls at him. He doesn't say a word, but I can feel the weight of his gaze, the way his stance straightens, his muscles tensing like he's suddenly alert.

I hold his gaze, steady and unblinking, knowing he's just as aware of what's happening between us as I am. There's a raw chemistry in the silence, and it's anything but polite.

"May I help you find anything, Captain Ashford?" Odette asks.

Gabriel turns to her and runs a hand through his hair. "I was hoping for a new coat," he gives me a sideways glance and says, "but I suppose I've found something better."

I roll my eyes. "Are you following me?"

"I had business in town, and I usually slip in here." His eyes drop to the dress I'm wearing, and he smiles. "Suits you well."

Before I can respond, he turns casually to Odette and says, "Put whatever she wants on my account."

I gasp. "You don't have to do that."

Gabriel gives me an easy smile. "I can't imagine you had much coin wash up with you when you found yourself stranded at sea."

I swallow hard, hoping my gratitude is clear in my voice. "Thank you, truly. I don't know how I'd manage without this."

His expression sharpens, and his voice is more serious now. "Listen. If you don't find anyone from your side before dusk, you need to get back to *The Tempest's Vow*. This city's no place to wander alone after dark. You could get hurt."

I hold his gaze, my voice steady despite the quickening in my chest. "I thought I wasn't invited back on the ship."

His eyes darken, and the faintest curve touches his lips. "That was before I saw you in that dress." His gaze lingers on the bodice for a moment, and then back to my face.

"I'm not sure if that's an invitation or a warning," I say, my voice low, matching his intensity.

"Perhaps both," he replies with mischief dancing in his eyes. "You will have to decide whether or not the danger aboard the ship or the danger of Port Royal suits you better, Miss Torres."

Gabriel addresses Odette. "Don't let her leave without at least half a dozen dresses." And with that, he turns away, his coat sweeping behind him as he strides toward the door. I thank him once more, and he tips his hat. The door shuts behind him with a soft thud.

Odette watches me, a slow, knowing smile playing on her lips. "Mon Dieu," she says, her voice thick with amusement and just a hint of envy. "Even an old lady can see the fire between you two. It's hotter than the sun beating down on the docks."

I tuck a loose strand of hair behind my ear, suddenly feeling exposed and strangely alive. "You really think so?"

She chuckles, shaking her head. "Ma cherie, I've seen many a pair pass through this door, but none with that sizzle and spark. Don't let it scare you. Set it ablaze."

I blush, and gather the dresses: silks and satins, pearls and lace—each one a world apart from the rough sea clothes I wore when I arrived. My fingers brush the fabric, and a small thrill runs through me knowing Gabriel offered to put them all on his tab.

Odette claps her hands softly. "Ah, monsieur is a generous one. You better go and enjoy yourself, ma belle. Whatever you do, make sure you find amusement. This city might be dangerous, but it's got its pleasures too."

Her words wash over me, and for the first time since the sea pulled me under, I decide to stop worrying and just have some damn fun.

DEVIL IN A BLUE DRESS

Gabriel

Sabrina is impossible not to notice. Even in a city full of noise and color, that dark blue and scandalously well-fitted dress moves like water when she walks. She's across the square now, weaving through the crowd. I shouldn't be watching her. I've got plenty I should be handling by now–coin to collect, men to threaten, information to pry loose before it slips away–but here I stand, still as stone, while she glides through the midday sun with those long gold-brown curls catching the light and making it damned hard to think straight.

She's curvier than most women, with fuller breasts, wider hips, and a backside so perfectly round, it's killing me. That dress doesn't just fit her. It worships her the way I should.

Stopping beside a stall, she pretends to study a length of ribbon, but I can tell she's not really looking at it. Her eyes dart past people, over shoulders, through crowds. She's searching, and I wonder who she's hoping to find first. A friend? That Navy father she mentioned? Someone who got dragged through the same storm she did?

Sabrina looks focused on her task, but the men in this city don't care who she's looking for. They only care how she looks, and right now, she looks like trouble worth chasing to the ends of the Earth.

I shift my stance, resting a hand on the hilt of my blade, resisting the ridiculous urge to cut down the next bastard who dares to stare at her too long, which is bloody ridiculous because she's not mine.

A sharp gust kicks dust into the air, and she turns her head, just a little, and I catch a flash of her profile. Her full lips, high cheekbones... God, I need to walk away. I have business to tend to before sundown, and I've already wasted too much time watching her.

I take one last look at the curve of her waist, the sway of her hips, the impossible way she makes a corset look like temptation incarnate, before I turn down the side alley.

I find the storehouse, reeking of gunpowder as usual. Salty air seeps in through the cracks in the wood, but it does nothing to chase the heat. The man across from me, Groier, wipes his brow with a grimy sleeve and squints down at the manifest I handed him.

"Twenty muskets, four crates of powder, thirty blades, and a dozen pistols with clean flints." He pauses. "That'll cost you."

I fold my arms. "You know I pay fairly, and I pay fast."

He grunts and scratches beneath his beard. "Aye, but this kind of haul makes a man ask questions. Planning a war, Ashford?"

"Something like it."

He doesn't press. Wise man. Port Royal is full of fools with loose mouths, but Groier isn't one of them, and that's why I've come to him. I don't need rumors, or worse, Royal Navy attention.

He marks off a few boxes on his sheet, then waves his hand toward the crates stacked near the back. "They'll be loaded into your hold before sunset. Quietly."

"I appreciate your discretion."

I leave him counting powder horns and stride across the narrow alley to the next stop: recruitment. My boots echo on the wooden planks as I push open the back door of the tavern, where men too rough for the front rooms spend their daylight hours drinking or nursing wounds. The ones I need are the kind that don't flinch at blood.

My first pick is already waiting. Horace, a towering brute with arms like tree trunks, leans against the wall with a tankard in one hand and a wicked grin on his face.

"Heard you were looking," he says.

"I am."

He tips back his drink and wipes his mouth. "This a quick job or the long kind?"

"The long kind. We're hunting a Spanish galleon. The *Mar de Sangre.*"

That gets his attention, and his grin vanishes. "The butcher ship."

I nod. "They didn't just take cargo. They took lives. My brother's. I'm getting them back, or sinking the bastard ship trying."

A few other heads turn, and I let the words hang in the air. The right men will hear them, and the ones who aren't right will go back to their drink.

"I'll come," Horace says. "For a share."

"You'll get plenty."

The room hums with tension and quiet determination as one by one, rough men, seasoned sailors, grizzled fighters, and restless mercenaries step forward. Each voice carries the same fierce resolve: they're in for the fight against the Spanish galleon, no questions asked. I watch them gather, sizing each man with sharp eyes, feeling the weight of the plan settling in.

When the last nod is given, I clap a heavy hand on the nearest man's shoulder, my voice low but steady. "We sail within the week. I'll send word. Prepare yourselves."

Without waiting for a response, I turn and slip into the main room of the tavern. The door closes behind me.

And there she is.

Sabrina sits alone at a battered table near the back, one hand curled loosely around a half-empty glass, the other tracing the rim. Her hair's down, wild from the wind, and even in this dim light she's impossible to miss… stunning, but not smiling.

A man's leaning too close, red-faced, bloated, stinking of ale and sweat so badly, I can smell him from across the room. He says something too low for me to catch, but whatever it is makes her freeze.

She forces a controlled smile. I can almost hear the words she's using to deflect, to defuse. I've seen that kind of poise before. It's the kind women learn when they're used to being cornered, but this bastard doesn't take the hint.

He plants a hand on the table and leans in closer. His other hand brushes her arm and lingers. Sabrina stiffens, then starts to rise, but he blocks her with his body, grinning like he's won.

That's enough.

Crossing the room, I barely register the clatter of a tankard falling or the startled glances thrown my way. His hand is on her shoulder now. She jerks away.

I grip the back of his collar and yank. He stumbles backward with a curse. I drive him into the wall hard enough to rattle the shelves. Bottles fall, and glass shatters.

"Take a walk," I say, low and cold.

His eyes widen. Recognition dawns, followed by the good sense to look terrified.

"I—I didn't mean any—"

"Be gone!"

He tries to sputter something else, but I step closer, and that ends it. He stumbles out, nearly tripping over a bench on the way, and the door slams behind him.

Silence settles as heads turn back to drinks.

I look at Sabrina. "You all right?" I ask.

She nods once, brushing a curl from her cheek. "It looks like I owe you another one."

"Owe me? I prefer to think of it as an investment in good company."

She blushes. "Is this the part where you remind me the city's no place for wandering women?"

"No," I murmur. "This is the part where I buy you another drink."

Sabrina slowly sinks back into her seat, and I call for two glasses and join her. I still don't know what to make of her. Her story's full of holes, and I don't trust how quickly she slipped under my skin. But I can't deny that when I saw that bastard's hand on her, something primal surged in me.

She's trouble, yes. She's got grit in her spine, fire in her eyes, and yet she's also adrift in a city that eats the careless alive. I don't make a habit of rescuing strange women, especially ones with more secrets than sense, but there's something about her that hits me in a place I thought had gone cold. God help me, Sabrina's a devil in a blue dress, and against my better judgement, I can't seem to walk away.

CHICKEN AND CHIVALRY

Gabriel slides into the chair across from me, his eyes darker in the dim light, and I hate that I notice every detail: the way his shirt hugs the line of his biceps, the way his jaw tightens when he focuses, and the quiet confidence that clings to him like the Caribbean heat. He never slouches or fidgets. He always moves like he owns the room, like every decision he makes is one step ahead of everyone else.

I take a deep breath. "Thank you for helping me. Again," I murmur, my fingers still wrapped around my half-empty glass. "Though I could've handled it."

"I have no doubt you could've," he says, not quite smiling. "But I figured I'd spare the man some bruises."

I laugh. "I appreciate that too. I wouldn't want to ruin my new dress."

"Precisely." He smiles. "Especially that one." His gaze lingers on my collarbone before traveling back up to my eyes.

He's the sexiest man I've ever met. Brave, tall, broad shoulders, quickwitted, and a voice like whiskey and sin. Normally, I'd be too busy wondering what his hands feel like or how it would feel if he kissed me, but today, I'm beyond tired.

My legs ache from walking, my throat's dry from asking questions that led nowhere, and Maddie is still missing. For all I know, she didn't get tossed into the seventeenth century and she's back home, enjoying electricity and a hot meal. And I hope she is. I don't know what I would do if I found out that she didn't survive the storm.

I set my glass down and lean back. "I spent all day combing this godforsaken port, and all I've got to show for it is a headache and some unwanted attention."

Gabriel's eyes don't move from mine. "Still searching for your people?"

"My sister," I correct him. "Basically. I've known her since we were nine. She's the only person who really knows me."

He nods slowly. "I'm sorry. I had no idea you were searching for your sister. You think she made it through the storm the same way you did?"

"I have to hope," I whisper. "If she didn't…." I trail off.

The silence stretches, heavy and intimate. Then he says, softer than I expect, "You're not alone, you know."

I glance up. "Aren't I?"

His jaw flexes, and he gently brushes his hand over mine. "You are not."

A barmaid sets down two fresh drinks, and I give her a grateful nod. The moment breaks. I lift the glass to my lips, grateful for the burn of the rum.

We finish our drinks. Gabriel watches me for a long moment, then asks, "Are you hungry?"

I manage a sheepish nod. "Starving."

He stands without a word, then glances at the packages on the table and scoops them up under one arm. "Come on."

Gabriel pays for our drinks, and I follow him out into the noisy street. He doesn't explain where we're going, and I don't ask.

The streets are still just as crowded and chaotic as they were midday, though the air is cooler, a soft breeze drifting through the narrow alleys of Port Royal. People pass us without notice, too busy drinking, trading, or shouting over barrels of fish.

Gabriel moves like he knows exactly where he's headed, turning left, then right, then ducking down a narrow lane so tight we have to turn sideways. The buildings lean toward each other overhead, their balconies almost touching, blocking most of the moonlight. I feel like I'm slipping between the ribs of the city, some hidden space that exists just outside the usual rhythm.

Finally, he stops at a door that doesn't look like much. It's weathered, gray, and set into what I'd swear was just a house. There's no sign or music.

He raps twice, then lifts a hand to the rusted handle. When the door creaks open, I expect a dusty, forgotten room, but the inside is quaint, lit by candles tucked into sconces and lanterns hanging low over tables. It's small, but the air smells like roasted meat, warm bread, and something faintly sweet, like spiced cider.

A few patrons murmur soft greetings to Gabriel from corners, eyes barely glancing up. The woman behind the bar gives him a knowing nod, then disappears through a back curtain.

"This place doesn't take strangers," he says simply, setting my packages down on a bench beside the table he chooses. "But I'm no stranger."

"No kidding." I slide onto the bench next to him.

"Kidding?" he asks, his brow furrowed, and I silently scold myself for remembering to have an accent, but not remembering that certain words are not used in this era.

"Jesting," I correct myself.

"Ah. Some of the phrases you use are incredibly foreign to me." He leans back, his arms draped across the top of the bench like he has all the time in the world. "Where did you say you grew up?"

"My sister and I grew up all over the world. I picked up different vernaculars and accents along the way," I say, lying through my teeth.

When the woman returns, she sets down a plate piled high with delicious smelling food. The chicken is roasted with herbs, the bread is still warm, the crust crackling as I tear it apart, and the potatoes are perfectly cooked, soaking up every bit of the rich gravy.

"God," I murmur. "I could cry."

Gabriel laughs as he lifts his wineglass. After only a few moments, his plate is nearly as empty as mine. Clearly, he's just as hungry, and the low sound he makes after another bite tells me he's enjoying it as much as I am.

Gabriel's left arm rests casually along the bench behind me, his body angled just slightly my way, close enough that I can feel the pull between us. He doesn't speak much, but when he does, it's with a sort of quiet satisfaction, commenting on the spices on the chicken or the softness of the bread, his voice like heat in the small space.

The wine is rich and dark, warming my chest and making it far too easy to forget how complicated this all is, and that's what throws me the most about Gabriel. His quiet kindness in the midst of chaos, and his patience. After everything I've seen in this century–shouting men, clashing swords, suspicious glares and too many hands reaching where they shouldn't–Gabriel's simple, thoughtful gestures hit harder than I expect.

The woman who made the food returns to the table just long enough to pour us each a cup of spiced ale. She gives Gabriel a knowing wink before disappearing again.

"What was that look?" I ask, sipping cautiously. It tastes like cinnamon and cloves.

"She likes me," he says.

"She feeds you like she raised you."

"She nearly did." He glances at the curtain she disappeared behind. "When I first came to Port Royal, I'd just lost everything. She gave me a meal and a place to sit. Been paying it back since."

I nod slowly, understanding more than I expected to. "Madame Rue is a good woman, and a damn fine cook."

"She is."

We lapse into a comfortable silence, and I lean back, just enough to brush against Gabriel's arm, toying with the idea of resting my head on his shoulder. I hesitate, still unsure how he'll react. His chivalrous English manners always seem to tangle with that untamed pirate spirit of his, keeping him from doing what I sometimes wish he would–devour me the way he did Madame Rue's roast chicken.

I glance at him sideways under the candlelight. There's a shadow of stubble along his strong jaw, and something dangerous in his eyes, even when he's sitting quiet and still. I know there's more to him than the swagger and steel. There's a protectiveness I didn't expect, and something inside me starts to ease.

The walk back to the ship is slow, and the cool night breeze whips my hair around in the darkness. Gabriel walks beside me, carrying the bundle of dresses tucked beneath one arm. His other hand swings loose at his side, close enough to brush mine a few times as we move through the quieter streets. Each time it happens, a spark shoots through me, and I hope he'll take the hint and close the distance, but he never does. His posture stays protective but contained, that gentlemanly restraint coiled tight beneath the pirate exterior, and it's maddening.

As we reach the edge of the docks, Gabriel slows and turns to face me. The wind pushes a few strands of hair across my face. He reaches out, his knuckles grazing my cheek as he brushes them back. His gaze holds mine, calm but intense, like he's deciding something.

His fingers hover near my skin a second longer than necessary. I hold still, waiting—hoping, but then he drops his hand and steps back half a pace. "We should keep moving," he says, his voice low. "It's late."

Frustrating! Maddening! But he makes me feel safe, and somewhere under the desire humming in my veins, I'm grateful.

When we board *The Tempest's Vow*, the deck is quiet, most of the crew off-duty or asleep. Lantern light glows faintly along the rigging. Gabriel leads me below, stopping just outside Isla's quarters, and hands me the packages.

He shifts, glancing down at me. "You need a bit of rest. I'll see if I can help you find your sister or your father tomorrow."

"Thank you," I say quietly. "For today. For everything."

I consider throwing my arms around him, but he nods once and turns away.

I lift my hand to knock, hesitating for just a breath before tapping lightly on the cabin door. The hinges creak as it opens almost instantly.

"Sabrina!" Isla's face lights up as she pulls the door wider. Her dark curls are tied back, her cheeks flushed like she's been laughing or arguing with Tomas, probably both.

Tomas appears behind her, his eyebrows lifting in surprise before he settles into a wide grin. "Well, look who survived the wilds of Port Royal," he says, stepping aside to let me in.

"I didn't know if you'd still be up," I say, slipping past them into the cozy little room.

"We were just talking," Isla says. "Mostly about you."

Tomas nods solemnly. "I said you were probably off charming half the island."

I roll my eyes, but I'm smiling. "More like being trampled by it."

Isla reaches for my hand and gives it a quick squeeze. "We're glad you're back. We missed you."

"I missed you both, too. Captain Ashford is allowing me to stay aboard another night. I looked everywhere but didn't find my family."

"You poor girl," Isla says, already pulling me toward the cot. "Tell me everything. Also, what *is* this bundle?"

I untie the dresses and hand her the pale green one with tiny silver buttons and gauzy sleeves. "For you."

Her eyes go wide. "No! Are you serious?"

"Of course. You gave me your clothes. I stretched your skirt in five directions. This is yours."

She grins, her cheeks flushed, and hurries off to try it on. When she reappears, she's stunning—like something out of a storybook. Tomas whistles and promptly earns a slap to the chest from her.

Eventually, I give Isla back her clothes, now folded neatly in the corner, and we all say our goodnights.

The ship rocks gently beneath me, like it's reminding me that time's still moving forward, even if I've landed in the wrong century. I think about Maddie. She's not walking the streets of Port Royal, or weaving through crowds or ducking into shops. If she had survived that storm, if she'd been pulled through time too... I would've found her by now.

She's still home, safe, and in the right century, probably tearing the world apart trying to find me. Honestly, it's the best possible place for her to be, because no matter how calm tonight feels, I know something is coming. This place, in this year, isn't safe. The earthquake is coming, and I don't want Maddie anywhere near it.

I exhale slowly, pulling the blanket up to my shoulders. The warmth of the meal, the laughter with Isla and Tomas, and the excitement of Gabriel's near-kiss, all swirl together, carrying me toward sleep.

GOD FORGIVE ME

GABRIEL

I wake before the sun, the sea wind already curling through the open slats in the wall, thick with salt and heat. The city outside stirs like a beast just starting to twitch in its sleep. Normally, this is my quiet hour where the world's still mine alone, where I can think, plan, sharpen the edge of whatever comes next, but I can't stop thinking about Sabrina.

That maddening woman with her long curly hair and bright hazel eyes, that dress that clung like it had secrets of its own, and her lips— God help me. I've met women all over the world, and none of them have ever entranced me like she has.

Sabrina's not like the other women, and that's the damned problem. She's tough, clever, but she's *not* built for what's coming….

I should've kissed her last night. *Every* fiber in me wanted to. There were a dozen moments when she leaned close, when her fingers brushed mine, when her laugh cracked something open in my chest, but I didn't.

I can't. Not when I'm sailing toward a Spanish galleon I intend to burn to the waterline, and not when I might not make it back.

And *definitely* not when one look at her tells me she's the kind of woman who'd follow you straight into the storm without hesitation. I can't and won't have that, and if I kiss her, it'll mean something. It'll *start* something, and I already know how that ends: with her in danger, maybe worse. The thought of her in that battle makes my gut twist in ways I don't want to admit.

I can't pull her into my mess. I can't give her even one more reason to stay tangled up with me, which means today, I will help her find whoever it is she's looking for—her sister, her father, her crew. I'll march through this cursed city and turn over every stone, every rumor, every tavern whisper until I know she has someone else to protect her, and then she's gone from my ship.

Sabrina's trouble. From the moment she walked into my life in that storm-soaked dress with her lies, her fire, and her damned stubborn tongue, she's been nothing but a complication of the worst kind.

The kind that makes a man start thinking of things other than revenge....

But I've waited too long for this fight. *The Mar de Sangre* is out there, floating like a phantom, waiting for me to come finish what they started.

So, I'll help her today. I'll do right by her, and then I'll let her go, and pray she doesn't give me one more reason to change my mind.

An hour or two after dawn, I knock on the door of the room Sabrina and Isla share. Sabrina opens the door, and for a moment, I forget how to breathe.

The gown she's wearing is a soft red, something between sunrise and firelight, and it fits her like it was sewn with her specifically in mind. The neckline dips just enough to make my blood stir, and the bodice hugs her curves in ways that make me jealous of the fabric. Her hair is down again, loose around her shoulders, and the morning sun turns it into gold.

She sees me staring and pauses, lifting a brow like she knows damn well what she's doing to me.

"You look lovely this morning," I say, because *God help me*, I can't *not* say something.

She laughs—a light, unexpected sound that catches in my chest and rattles something loose. And there it is again: that pull toward her. That cursed, constant ache. "Thank you," she says. "You look handsome this morning as well."

I offer her my arm. "Come on. Let's find your family."

We spend the morning walking Port Royal from end to end. The city has always had a pulse, loud and erratic, but today it feels like background noise to her voice as she questions merchants, soldiers, dockworkers... anyone who might've seen her sister, or a Navy man matching her father's description.

They all give the same answer: a shake of the head, a polite sorry, a half-interested shrug.

She's relentless, brave, and smart. She asks questions, watches faces, and presses people for information like she's chasing ghosts. At least, that's what I tell myself. I want to believe she's still hunting for her sister, her father—any trace of the family she claims she's lost.

But sometimes, when she pauses by a weathered building or studies a bustling street vendor with more curiosity than urgency, I catch a flicker of something else in her eyes. It's like she's seeing the city for the first time, not as a desperate refugee searching for lost kin, but as someone trying to find a place to belong.

I lead her through the crooked alleys near the west port, where ships fly flags I don't recognize, and the shadows hold more secrets than the sunlit streets. The men here aren't friendly, but she doesn't flinch. She moves beside me calmly, asking about this ship, that market, a whispered story of sailors and smugglers.

Her questions are pointed, yes, but not always about people. Sometimes she lingers on the details as if she's soaking in the city itself.

I watch her closely, and she keeps up the story, talking about Maddie, her father, her past, but in her eyes, there's a distance that makes me wonder if she's clinging to those names because they're all she has left to hold on to—not because she believes she'll find them here.

Still, I don't press her. If she's lost hope, she doesn't show it outright. For now, she's still searching. Or at least, that's what she wants me to believe, and I'll walk beside her, whether she's hunting family or just looking for a place to breathe.

When the sun's high, I lead her into a shaded tavern tucked behind a tailor's shop. We share cold water, whiskey, and crusty bread, and she leans back, exhausted.

"Nothing," she murmurs. "It's like they vanished."

I say nothing. There's a chance, God, there's a *good* chance they didn't survive that storm. She's alone, and she knows it. She's just not ready to say it aloud yet.

We rest, then head back out, searching the markets, the Navy yards, the outlying camps near the forts where survivors sometimes land. We even stop at the church, and she leaves her name with the parish clerk, just in case someone comes looking.

By the time the sky starts to glow gold and the shadows stretch long across the dirt streets, we've found nothing. No sister. No father. Just the quiet ache of disappointment tightening in her shoulders.

But she still smiles at me when I ask if she wants to head back. She nods, and I offer her my arm again. This time she takes it without hesitation, like it's the most natural thing in the world. We walk the rest of the way in silence, her presence at my side both grounding and distracting.

When we reach the ship, I hand her off to Isla and Tomas. They greet her with warmth and laughter, and I let myself believe, for a moment, that she's safe here, at least for now.

But I don't follow them below deck. I need a moment to think, breathe, and put some space between this woman and the storm she's stirring in my chest.

* * *

I've been pacing my study for half an hour, working through the words I know I need to say. They're all perfectly logical, and necessary, but they all feel like hell.

When Sabrina knocks, I nearly forget how to breathe. She steps in slowly, her eyes sweeping the room. "You wanted to see me?"

I nod once and gesture toward the small table set beside the windows. "I thought you might be hungry."

She arches an eyebrow but walks in, taking a seat. That red dress she's still wearing clings to her in ways that aren't helping my ability to think clearly, and her hair is pinned up loosely now, little strands curling around her face.

"You're feeding me again," she says, amused. "That's becoming a habit."

"I like making sure you eat," I reply, sitting across from her. "There's not much else I can offer."

She picks up her fork. "I think I'll allow it."

We eat in silence for a while—Madame Rue's done something incredible with roast pork and some sweet bread that's still warm. Every time Sabrina sighs contentedly, it twists something in my chest.

She takes a sip of the wine I poured, then meets my eyes over the rim. "All right, Captain. Out with it."

I blink. "Out with what?"

"That thing you've been brooding about all day."

Of course, she noticed. I set my cup down, push back from the table, and walk to the window, bracing both hands on the sill. "We leave the day after tomorrow."

"For what?"

"For war," I say. "The *Mar de Sangre*. She's been sighted near an inlet east of here. We're going after her."

Her chair scrapes the floor as she rises. "Is that the ship that attacked your brother's vessel?"

"Yes, we are going to ambush them the way they did James. Sabrina, I want you off this ship before we set sail."

Her mouth opens in protest, but I keep going. "I'll find you safe lodging in town. I'll pay the rent myself, but you won't be on this ship."

Her jaw tightens. "Because I'm a woman?"

"Because you *matter* to me," I snap. "And I don't want to see you hurt or dead."

Her expression softens just a fraction. "You think I haven't lived through danger?"

"I think you haven't lived through what I'm about to start."

"I was thrown into the sea during a storm so violent it could've torn the world in two," she says, her voice low but even, as she steps toward me. "I nearly drowned. You don't get to treat me like I'm some delicate thing that needs tucking away while the real work happens."

She moves closer to me, her eyes fierce. "I can pull my weight. I *will*. There'll be blood. I know that, but if you're hurt, Gabriel, if something happens to you, and I'm not there…." Her voice breaks, just slightly. "Don't shut me out to protect me. Let me stay. Let me fight beside you."

"I'm trying to keep you *alive*, Sabrina!"

She looks up at me, her breath shallow, her cheeks flushed with heat and anger. Sabrina crosses the room, lifts a hand, and curls her fingers against my shirt. "I didn't ask you to protect me."

Her lips part, her breath brushes my jaw, and *God help me*, I know I'm going to kiss her.

My hands find her waist as she rises on her toes. Her mouth meets mine in a rush of heat and want. Not soft or delicate, but a collision. A final confession, and a goddamn unraveling. I kiss her like I'll never get the chance again. By the time we break apart, we're both breathless.

"I'm still not leaving," she whispers.

I shut my eyes. "You should," I whisper back.

"I'm staying."

I let the truth of that settle. If she stays behind in Port Royal alone, she could be in just as much danger, but if she's on my ship when the cannon fire starts, there may not be a second chance. Not for her. Not for me. But I don't have it in me to fight her anymore, and a woman who offers to go to battle at your side is a woman worth keeping.

I brush a hand through her hair, and let my thumb trace her cheek.

"Then stay."

God forgive me.

MAR DE SANGRE

I push open the door to our cramped quarters, the wood creaking softly, and spot Isla sitting on the narrow bunk, her dark eyes flicking up from the book she's reading. Tomas is sprawled on the floor, fiddling with some knots on a coil of rope.

"This is going to be the death of me," Tomas mutters, glancing up as I step in. "I swear, every knot's a puzzle."

Isla laughs quietly, tucking a stray curl behind her ear. "You'll get there, Tomas. Just takes time."

I pause in the doorway, my chest tightening with the rush of words I'm about to say—news too big for this small room. But it needs to be said. I can't keep this secret tucked away any longer.

"He kissed me," I blurt out, surprising even myself with how loud it sounds in the stillness.

Isla blinks then sets the book aside, her eyes huge and curious. Tomas freezes mid-knot, his gaze shooting to me like I've just dropped a bomb.

"Who kissed you?" Tomas asks, voice a little too eager.

"Gabriel," I say, my voice soft. "We kissed."

The room feels charged all at once. Tomas's jaw drops, but there's a smile dancing behind his eyes, and Isla looks just as shocked.

"Well," Isla says after a beat, "that's something you don't hear every day aboard a ship."

I take a deep breath and move to sit on my cot. "I didn't plan it. It just happened. There's this pull, something I can't explain. He's not like anyone I've ever met. He's so sexy, so commanding, and also so protective."

Isla nods. "He's a complicated man."

"You think?" I mutter with a half-smile.

Tomas flashes a grin. "Looks like you're sticking around longer than you thought, and honestly, I'm glad. The ship's a lot livelier with you on it."

I stare at the wooden planks beneath my feet, thinking about the danger looming over us, the *Mar de Sangre*, the Spanish galleon we're meant to fight. Gabriel's already told me he wants me off the ship before the battle, but something in me refuses to leave.

"Yes. I'm staying," I say quietly, almost more to myself than to them. "Not just because of him but because of this ship. It feels safer than the chaos outside. Port Royal is wild and dangerous, and I don't have anyone there. But here, with Gabriel, and the two of you... I have friends. I have a place."

"We're glad to have you. It's not easy, being alone in a city like that," Isla says.

"No," I agree. "And I want to protect you both. I can't let anything happen to you. If the battle's coming, we have to look out for each other."

"The captain told you about the Spanish, I take it?" Tomas asks.

I nod, solemnly.

"We're a crew, whether by blood or by choice," he adds.

"And I want to be part of that. I don't want to be just a passenger anymore. I want to be part of this, part of what happens next."

Isla squeezes my hand. "And you will be. We'll make sure of it."

Tomas grins, the knot forgotten. "Besides, a ship's got room for all kinds of troublemakers."

I laugh. "Thank you."

"For what?" Isla asks, tilting her head.

"For accepting me."

Isla shrugs, but there's warmth in her eyes. "That's what friends do."

I lay back against the bunk, the weight in my chest easing just a little. Outside this tiny room, the world waits, unpredictable and wild. But here, with Gabriel and these two, I have something worth fighting for.

Before long, the creak of the hull and the slap of water against the side of the ship settles into a rhythm that's strangely comforting. The lantern swings above, casting slow, golden arcs across the wooden walls. Isla's already asleep, breathing softly in the bunk across from mine, and Tomas is likely off making mischief or snoring somewhere in a hammock.

I'm wide awake, staring at the ceiling, trying to process the fact that tomorrow I'll be aboard a battleship. Not just sailing, but sailing into danger, into an actual fight with cannons, smoke, and blood.

I should be curled up in a rented room in Port Royal, pretending to search for a family that doesn't exist, and trying to prepare for the ground to crack open. But the thought of being out there alone is worse than facing whatever comes next with Gabriel, Tomas, and Isla. They're not strangers from another century anymore. They're my people, as crazy and impossible as that sounds.

I don't know what's going to happen tomorrow. I don't know who we'll lose or if we'll win. But I do know one thing: I'd rather face battle with Gabriel than face the alternative alone.

I don't even know what to call what's happening between us—a spark, a pull, a storm brewing under the surface. He *finally* kissed me tonight. I can still feel the warmth of his hands on my waist, the brush of his lips on mine, the way he looked at me like he'd been holding back for far too long.

I want to believe that was real. I want to believe he meant it, and even if he didn't say the words, I saw it in his eyes. He cares.

So I'm staying. For Isla and Tomas because they've become my only friends in this wild world. For the ship, which somehow feels safer than the city ever could. But mostly, for him, because I want to be loyal to Gabriel, to repay him for his kindness.

* * *

The morning of the raid dawns far too bright, the sun climbing over Port Royal like it doesn't know lives will be lost before it sets again. I stand at the rail, my fingers curled tightly around the worn wood as the crew rushes past me, sharpening blades, checking powder, knotting ropes with practiced hands. The usual banter is gone. There's only the thrum of urgency and the clicking of cannon hatches opening.

Tomas checks his pistol and grins at me with too much bravado. "Stay low. Don't get killed," he says. Isla is near the mast, her expression serious as she tucks a small dagger into her boot.

Gabriel presses a cold, heavy pistol into my hand, the weight unfamiliar but somehow grounding. Then he slips a dagger into my belt, its worn leather sheath rough against my fingers. "You may need these if they make it aboard," he says quietly. "Stay close, and keep your wits."

My heart races, but I nod, clutching the weapons. Surely they won't make it aboard. Our cannons will do the job.

We sail for hours, and when the Spanish galleon finally appears on the horizon, something in the crew seems to freeze, like breath being held.

The *Mar de Sangre* cuts through the haze like a beast, its black-and-red sails billowing like wings. For one suspended moment, we all watch it creep closer.

Then we fire a single cannon shot, and the deck erupts. Everything becomes chaos, fire, smoke, and screaming. The ship jerks beneath my feet as shots slam into her side.

The thunder of cannon fire rolls across the water, rattling my bones as I cling to the rail and watch the chaos unfold. The Spanish are coming hard and fast, their longboats slicing through the waves, their oars moving quickly as they row toward us with ruthless precision.

Our crew fires as quickly as they can, muskets cracking, pistols sparking, the acrid smell of powder hanging thick in the air, but the enemy keeps coming, relentless, ducking low and pushing through the spray. I can see the gleam of metal at their sides, swords and pistols ready, and hear the shouted orders in a language I barely understand.

The first boat slams into our hull, and then another. We end many of them, their bodies falling lifeless into the sea. But before anyone can stop them, figures are already scaling the sides of *The Tempest's Vow*, grappling hooks flying, as they haul themselves aboard with terrifying speed.

We shoot, we slash, we try to drive them back, but they keep coming, leaping over the rails. The battle is no longer out there on the sea. It's here, on the deck, and there's nowhere left to run.

Shouts ring out in English and Spanish, overlapping and confusing. I cower behind a stack of barrels and watch two men go at each other with sabers, moving so fast I can barely follow. One is ours, the other Spanish. They circle, their blades sparking, with curses flying. The Spanish man lands a cut to the shoulder, but the *Vow* crewman kicks him back and finishes it with a final, brutal swing.

Gunfire cracks nearby. I spin toward the sound. Tomas stands near the helm with a pistol in each hand. He fires once, then again, dropping two Spanish boarders before they can make it across the deck. But, he doesn't stop to gloat. He reloads fast, his face pale but focused.

Movement to my left draws my attention, and I turn just in time to see Elias locked in combat. He knocks back his attacker, drives him toward the mainmast, and I almost think he'll win. I want to believe it, but then, behind him, a second Spaniard emerges from the smoke. Elias doesn't see him. He's too focused. I scream as the blade flashes. I see it happen: a quick arc and then Elias stumbles, clutching at his neck, blood spilling between his fingers. His sword drops to the deck, and his body follows.

I don't move, and I can't breathe. The world narrows to that sight, that sound, the awful reality that Elias is gone. Stumbling back, I nearly trip over a crate and catch myself just as another wave of Spanish sailors floods the deck. I turn wildly, looking for Gabriel, Isla, Tomas, for anyone.

Isla's crouched near the port rail, pistol out, but she's cornered. A Spanish sailor, young, tall, bloodied, advances on her with a blade raised high. She fires, but the shot misses. He snarls something I don't understand and lunges.

She tries to scramble back, but her heel catches and she goes down hard. He looms over her, his blade ready, and her hands come up instinctively, too late to stop it.

I don't think; I just shoot.

He gasps, a sharp inhale of disbelief. His body stiffens, and for a second, his eyes meet mine, wide with shock. Then he collapses forward, lifeless.

The silence that follows is brief and brutal. I hear myself breathing too fast. My pulse pounds in my ears. Isla scrambles up beside me, her eyes darting between me and the man at our feet. I can't stop staring at the blood. Everything feels distant and unreal.

And then the chaos dies down around us. I kneel beside the body long after the danger is gone.

The cannon fire has stopped, and the shouting fades. Still, I stay here, kneeling next to the body of the man whose life I took. The gun lies on the deck beside me, useless now.

I saved Isla. I know that, but the gravity of what I've done crashes into me, heavy and raw. My stomach twists. I want to forget it, and I know I never will.

Footsteps echo across the bloodied deck, boots splashing through the pooling water and spilled rum. I don't look up until a familiar voice cuts through the ringing in my ears.

"Sabrina?"

Gabriel stands there, blood running down one arm, a slice cut through the fabric of his shirt and a smear of soot across his jaw. His eyes find mine, searching, desperate. When he sees that I'm whole, he lets out a gasp. Without a word, he crouches and gathers me into his arms.

I don't resist. I press my face to his shoulder, my fingers curling into the back of his shirt as I try not to fall apart. He holds me tighter, and the war still rages inside my head.

"I killed him," I whisper. "I didn't think—I just moved. He would've killed her."

"I know," he says softly. "You did what you had to do."

I pull back just far enough to see his face. "Elias…."

His jaw clenches, and he nods once. "I saw."

We're both quiet for a moment, the reality of it settling between us. The dead are being wrapped in linen. We tend to the wounded where they lie. Tomas passes by, limping and clutching a bandaged arm. He gives me a small nod, and Isla catches my eye too, from across the deck. She presses a hand to her heart. I don't know if she's thanking me or checking that she's still alive. Maybe both.

"We won," Gabriel says roughly. "The *Mar de Sangre* is ours, what's left of her. The treasure hold is full. We'll divvy it up once the smoke clears."

"You're bleeding," I say, brushing a thumb over the torn sleeve of his shirt.

"I've had worse injuries."

"I thought we might die."

"So did I." He smiles faintly, then cups my cheek with his good hand. "You're safe now."

I lean into his touch, trembling. The sky above us is softening to twilight, streaked with fire and ash. The sea rocks beneath our feet, and for now, at least, we are alive, and together.

LOYALTY AND LUST

The deck is quieter now, but it's not peaceful. Smoke still lingers in the air, and the scent of blood clings to everything. My ears ring from cannon fire, and every breath feels like a struggle against ash and salt.

Men move around me, some limping, others with bandaged arms or shoulders, their faces streaked with soot and blood. A few of them nod when they pass me, not quite smiling, just acknowledging. I'm not just cargo anymore. I'm someone who fought—someone who *killed*.

Beside me, Isla crouches with a wet cloth, helping an older crewman bind a gash along his leg. She glances over her shoulder at me. "I still can't believe it," she says quietly.

I swallow. "That I killed someone?"

"No. That you saved my life." Her voice catches, and for a moment she stops what she's doing. "You didn't even hesitate. Thank you, Sabrina."

In the moment, something deeper than instinct took over. Instinct would've told me to run. This was something else. This was loyalty and love.

I crouch beside her, grabbing a roll of bandages. "I'm glad you're safe."

She leans in and squeezes my hand, a brief, sisterly gesture in the midst of so much pain.

Across the deck, they're lifting Elias's body in a linen shroud. I can't watch for long, looking away before they release his body into the sea. Even though we had our differences, Elias was a good man, and a tremendously loyal first mate. He will be missed by everyone aboard *The Vow*, especially Gabriel.

Gabriel, who can't watch either, shouts an order from the quarter-deck, his voice hoarse. "Secure the mainsail! Rig for repairs! Tend the wounded!" He moves stiffly, favoring his left arm, but his voice doesn't waver.

Crewmembers swarm across the ship. Some lower lifeboats to retrieve what they can from the Spanish galleon. Others are already boarding it, carrying sacks of coin, weapons, crates of powder and preserved food back. I glance toward the other ship. The *Mar de Sangre* tilts slightly in the water, her rigging torn and sails burned through.

Once she's empty, Gabriel gives the final order. "Light it."

One of the men tosses a torch, and flames lick up the shattered wood like they've been waiting. Within minutes, the Spanish galleon is burning.

I watch it from the stern, my arms crossed tight over my chest. I don't know whether I feel relief, guilt, or both. Maybe I'm not ready to feel anything yet.

Gabriel moves toward me, his silhouette cut sharp against the glow of the flames. With each step, the tension in my shoulders begins to loosen, the tight coil of nerves in my stomach unspooling. There's something about the calm, grounded way he carries himself that makes the reality of this moment feel a little less overwhelming, and a little more bearable.

"Your crew held their own," I say.

"Revenge is a hell of a motivator. You were brave today."

"I killed a man."

"You saved a life."

"I still killed someone," I say, louder this time. "I didn't freeze. I didn't scream. I just—pulled the trigger."

"Sabrina, you had to. You did well."

I turn to him now and really look at him. There's blood dried near the corner of his mouth, a rip in his shirt, and bruises blooming across his chest. He looks like he's been through hell.

"I thought it would be different," I admit. "I assumed there'd be some cannon fire, and one of the ships would go down. In my mind, either we'd drown or they would, and I was ready to fight the ocean again. But I never allowed myself to imagine hand-to-hand combat, with real guns and swords. Nor did I ever think *I* would have to *kill* someone."

"I shouldn't have let you come. You should be at the port right now, safe and secure," he says. "And now you'll carry this for the rest of your life. It's my fault. I'm sorry, Sabrina."

I swallow hard. "I volunteered to come. I'm glad I did. Isla...."

"Isla might not be here if you hadn't been." He looks out toward the last smoldering sparks of the enemy ship.

I follow his gaze and wonder if by saving Isla, I may have just changed some small part of history.

"So what about you, Captain? Did you get what you came for?"

"I got justice. Or something of that nature."

We watch the flames together. The sea catches the firelight, throwing back glints of gold and orange. I wonder if that ship held someone's brother. Someone's son. I wonder if the man I killed had someone waiting at home for him.

The wind shifts, and Gabriel turns and starts shouting instructions again. The crew works to set the sails and plot a course back to Port Royal. Even the injured are up, helping where they can. No one's slacking, not today. Not after the price we paid.

The deck is still stained with blood. A torn flag flaps overhead, and Tomas limps across the quarterdeck carrying a crate full of coins, grinning through a split lip.

We won, and we survived. I'm still standing, but I'm not the same woman who boarded this ship, and I never will be again.

As the last light of day stains the sky in rusty golds, we gather in a hushed circle, mugs of rum and ale in hand. The flames that consumed the Spanish ship are now embers on the horizon, and our own vessel rocks gently, battered but intact. Someone holds a lantern at the center of our gathering, its warm glow flickering against tired, bloodied faces.

One by one, crew members murmur names of the fallen. A few offer short prayers. Others just stand in silence, hats in hand. I catch sight of Tomas with a fresh bandage around his arm, his eyes downcast. Isla is next to me, her fingers laced in mine.

Gabriel steps forward, looking around at all of us, and then beyond us, into the darkening sky. When he finally speaks, his voice carries low and clear, heavy with something rawer than grief.

"Elias Finch was a thorn in my side from the moment I made him first mate," Gabriel says. A few people smile through their sadness. "He was stubborn, argumentative, and always thought he was right— which, to his credit, he often was— he was loyal and brave. He was the kind of man who didn't flinch when things turned ugly."

Gabriel pauses, his jaw tightening, and takes a deep breath. "He saved my life more than once. He died fighting for this ship—for all of us—and I'll carry those debts the rest of my life. To Elias Finch," he finishes, raising his mug.

We all echo softly and solemnly. "To Elias Finch."

The sun slips beneath the horizon in streaks of burnt orange and violet, and the sea turns black and endless around us. The ship is quieter now, full of hushed voices. We have buried the bodies at sea, stitched and wrapped the wounded, and half-mended torn sails. A few men hum soft shanties while they finish the work, and someone plays a slow, mournful tune on a fiddle.

Gabriel finds me just after nightfall and offers his good arm. I take it without question.

His quarters are dimly lit by a single oil lamp swaying from a hook, shadows crawling along the walls as the ship rocks gently beneath our feet. He gestures toward the table, where a bottle of rum and two battered tin cups wait. I nod and sit on his bed while he pours.

We drink in silence at first. The rum is sharp, burning down my throat and spreading warmth through my belly. I let the heat settle there, watching him as he leans his shoulder against the wall.

"James would've liked you," he says at last. "You're brave. Clever, too. You notice things most people miss. You ask questions, you think things through… and you're kind," he adds after a moment. "Even after everything you've been through, and all you've lost, you try to help people. You could've stayed in Port Royal this morning, but you came and fought instead."

A lump rises in my throat. "I wanted to show you how much your kindness and generosity mean to me."

He crosses the room and sinks down beside me on the edge of the bed, his voice gravelly with emotion. "I've been wanting to show you what you mean to me, Sabrina."

I don't know what to do with the ache in his voice, or the way it catches something in me and holds it tight. He brushes a thumb over my jaw as his other hand settles lightly on my hip, warm through the thin fabric. "You're the woman who saved a life today. You stood your ground and fought like hell. I saw you, and I'm proud of you." His voice is lower now, rougher, closer.

I feel it everywhere. My heart thuds wildly in my chest, and I suddenly realize how close we are. His scent—smoke and leather, wraps around me, and his gaze burns into mine.

I slide my hands up over his chest, feeling the heat beneath his shirt, the steady rhythm of his breath. He exhales slowly, like he's trying to keep himself from losing control.

I want him to lose control.

I kiss him, and he responds instantly. The hand he had on my hip moves to the small of my back, pulling me flush against him, the other cradling the back of my head. His mouth is fierce and tender all at once, all the tension between us finally igniting. He kisses me like he's been starving for it, like he doesn't care that the world was just on fire outside these walls.

I gasp against his lips, and he takes that sound as a challenge, deepening the kiss, then moving his lips to my neck and then my collarbone.

I tilt my head back and press my body closer to his, slipping my hands beneath the open folds of his shirt, skimming the warm, taut skin of his chiseled chest with my fingertips.

He draws in a sharp breath, as if my touch startles something inside him, and I feel him tense before he exhales. His hands are firmer now, settling at my waist, his thumbs sweeping small circles over the thin fabric of my dress.

He kisses the edge of my jaw, my throat, the hollow beneath my ear, and every brush of his mouth sends shivers racing down my spine.

"You drive me mad," he murmurs against my skin. "You have from the moment I laid eyes on you."

I smile through a rush of nerves and want. "That makes two of us."

Gabriel unlaces the top of my gown with careful fingers, pausing as though giving me a chance to stop him, but I don't. He pulls my dress over my head, and I pull him back to me. He lowers his head, kissing the newly exposed skin with aching tenderness, gliding his hands along my sides, over my waist, and up my ribs, stirring a quiet storm beneath my skin. When he takes my breasts in his hands and teases my nipples, I feel like I'm aflame beneath his touch.

"Take off your clothes," I beg in a whisper.

He wastes no time revealing his gorgeous sun bronzed body to me. I'm careful not to touch his fresh wounds, but the rest of his chiseled body is fair game.

I squeeze his biceps as he slides between my legs. He enters me, deliciously filling me with his thick member. The head of his cock rubbing my clit with every stroke, while Gabriel's lips wrap around my nipples. The passion, the ecstasy, and the undeniable connection we have, are too much for me to hold.

When release comes, it feels like a tide breaking, powerfully beautiful, sweeping through me in waves. My body arches toward him, every nerve lit with sensation.

Gabriel follows moments later, his body pressed close, his breath stuttering against my neck. There's something unguarded in the way he shudders, something raw and masculine that makes my chest ache. He buries his face in the crook of my shoulder as if the moment is almost too much to bear.

For a while, we don't speak, our bodies tangled in the warmth of each other. Gabriel's hand finds mine beneath the blanket. His fingers wrap around mine, rough and sure, and I squeeze back, silently promising that whatever comes next, we'll face it together.

RIDDLES

GABRIEL

The hour is still dark, in that silence just before the first gull cries. I lie awake, one arm draped around Sabrina's waist, her bare back warm against my chest. She shifts just slightly, a soft sound escaping her lips. It's not quite a word but more like a whisper from a dream.

Then, she says, "No… don't go down there. There's no signal…."

I don't move. *Signal?*

Her voice changes in her sleep. Her tone is still soft but strange, and she's speaking in a dialect I've never heard. The vowels stretch oddly, the Rs too hard, and the words are foreign. Yet, she says them again. It's clearer this time, something about *charging cables* and *low battery*. I don't know what those things are, but the tone is urgent, like a warning.

Another word follows, unfamiliar and sharp—*elevator*. She mutters it like it's a common, every day, word.

I hold still, barely breathing, as her brow creases, and she turns slightly in her sleep. I don't want to wake or scare her, but every instinct in me flares. Not from fear, but from the gnawing certainty that something about her isn't what it seems.

She's quiet again, exhaling softly. She's not a spy. I've ruled that out. She knows too little about the sea for that. And she's not faking these uncommon words—not with the way her body tenses, the way her voice catches like she's lived those dreams before.

I press a kiss to the crown of her head. Whatever world she comes from, I'm not going to wake her to ask. She's earned her rest.

But I *will* ask her in the morning, over coffee and eggs. I need to know because, despite the strangeness, I'm more certain than ever that Sabrina doesn't belong here, and yet, I don't want her anywhere else.

The warmth of Sabrina beside me is grounding, but my thoughts drift to Elias. I see his face every time I close my eyes. That crooked grin when he challenged me. The way he muttered under his breath when he disagreed, always thinking he knew better, and too often being right. He was the one I trusted with everything, even when I pretended I didn't. Not only was he my best friend, Elias was my anchor when the weight of the ship got too heavy. He knew my moods, my silences, and how to weather both.

I press my knuckles to my mouth, stifling the grief. There's no time to mourn when you command a ship, but the ache doesn't wait for permission. It lingers in my chest like sea rot, slow and relentless.

The sky begins to pale outside the porthole. I shift onto my side and watch her, just for a moment. Her brow is smooth again. The odd words have faded back into sleep. One hand curls under her cheek, her lips slightly parted. She looks peaceful, despite everything.

As the sun rises higher, she stirs with a soft sound, her lashes fluttering. "Is it morning?" she whispers, still half asleep.

"Nearly," I say, my voice low. "You were talking in your sleep."

That catches her attention. Her eyes open fully, searching mine.

"Unfamiliar words," I add. "Ones I didn't recognize."

Sabrina pauses as though she's mulling over what I've said. She doesn't deny it, but her expression folds into something unreadable. I let it lie—for now.

* * *

Later, in the galley, the scent of eggs and fried plantain hangs in the warm air. I sit across from her, one arm braced on the table, a mug of coffee cooling at my side.

She glances at me over her own mug, her eyes sharper now... awake, alert, but not entirely at ease.

"About what I said in my sleep—" she begins.

"I'm not pressing," I cut in. "I just... listened because I had no choice, and I noticed how strange many of the words were."

She sets her mug down. "It's complicated."

"Most things worth knowing are."

We eat quietly for a few moments. The ship creaks around us, and distant voices call out above deck. The crew is awake, wounded or not, drawn by the routine of survival. But down here, it's just the two of us, and something between us that wasn't here yesterday.

Finally, I ask, "Why do you refuse to tell me anything about your past?"

"I know you're curious," she says carefully. "And I wish I could explain everything, but I can't. Not yet."

Not yet.

The words land harder than they should. I study her face—those eyes that always seem to carry more than they let on, that mouth I kissed just hours ago. Alas, after everything, she's *still* holding back.

"You trust me with your life. You've slept in my bed. You've stood at my side in battle, but you can't tell me who you are?"

Her gaze falls to her plate. "It's not that I don't trust you—"

"Then what is it?" My voice rises more than I intend. "I've mourned beside you. Told you things I haven't spoken aloud in years."

"Gabriel—"

"No." I stand, pacing a short line across the galley floor, the worn boards creaking beneath my boots. "I've known thieves more forthcoming. Spies more honest. You say you're not a danger, that you're not lying, but you've wrapped your truths in riddles since the day you came aboard."

She's silent now, watching me, her arms wrapped around her middle like she's trying to keep herself from unraveling, and perhaps I understand. Perhaps I even sympathize, but I can't carry all of this alone.

"I can't be the only one baring their soul here, Sabrina," I say, quieter now, but more raw. "I won't beg for scraps of your truth while offering you all of mine." She opens her mouth, but I shake my head. "No more."

I grab the now empty mug and set it down harder than I should. "We're docking in Port Royal soon. I need a clear head if I'm going to bring this ship in safely."

"Gabriel, please—"

"You've earned your place, but I can't... I can't keep reaching for someone who won't reach back."

Her face falls, but she doesn't stop me when I walk past her and head for the ladder. The morning sun is cresting over the harbor, casting gold across the deck. The crew is moving again, alive with the momentum of survival. I climb the ladder, the wind cool against my face.

If she wants to tell me the truth, she will. Until then, I'll be her captain, not her lover.

And I'll keep my damn distance.

HIDING THE TRUTH

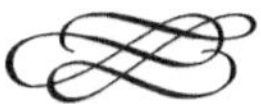

Sabrina

The room is quiet except for the soft creak of the hull and the distant hum of the crew above. I sit on the edge of the narrow cot in the room I share with Isla, my knees pulled up to my chest, my arms wrapped tightly around them. She's somewhere topside, probably helping with dock prep, and pretending not to notice I'm missing. I should be helping, too, but I can't move.

My body remembers everything: the way he touched me, the way he whispered my name. I gave myself to him without hesitation, and without fear. That's never happened before with anyone. I've never wanted it to, but with Gabriel, I submitted completely.

I press my forehead to my knees. My throat burns, and I feel weak. Now he thinks I'm a liar. I should have known better. I knew this would happen eventually—knew the questions would come, the ones I couldn't answer. But I didn't expect him to look at me like that. Like I was some stranger who'd betrayed him. After everything we've been through, after the storm, the city, the battle. And after last night...

I close my eyes and let the silence stretch around me. The truth claws at my throat. I want to tell him. I want to say: *I'm not from this world. Not from your century. I don't belong here.* But how do I even begin? What if he doesn't believe me? Or worse—what if he does?

He thinks I don't trust him, but I do. I trust him more than I've ever trusted anyone, and that's the part that hurts the most. The part of me that lives in reason says: *Stay quiet. You'll lose him if you say it out loud.* But the part that aches for him says: *You can tell him anything. You can trust him.*

What if this is the only real connection I ever get in this life? What if Gabriel is the only person I was ever meant to find—across centuries, across oceans? What if I keep this secret buried, and it ruins us anyway?

A tear slides down my cheek before I can stop it. I wipe it away with the back of my hand, furious at myself. I've faced storms, pirates, gunfire, death, and now I'm crumbling because the one person I let in decided I wasn't honest enough.

He's right. Of course I've been holding back, but I didn't know I'd fall in love with him. The truth may destroy what we have, but keeping it from him might, too.

I take a shaky breath. I don't know what I'm going to do, but one way or another, I can't keep this secret much longer.

A gull cries overhead, sharp and distant, and it cuts through the quiet like a warning. I lift my head just as boots thunder past the doorway, someone shouting too fast for me to catch the words. The world is moving again, even if I'm not, even if part of me wants to stay right here in this suspended moment where no decision has been made yet. Where Gabriel's voice isn't still echoing in my chest, hard-edged and cold. Where last night hasn't been buried under the weight of this morning.

And then the call rings out, clear and undeniable: "Land ho!"

I blink slowly, as if waking from a deep sleep. My heart stutters.

Port Royal.

I rise on unsteady feet and cross to the small porthole. The sea outside glints in the sun, endless blue bleeding into the curved edge of a pale sky. And there, just ahead, the smudge of land comes into view. Not just a shadow on the horizon now, but real, tangible and close.

Port Royal is louder than the sea, even before we dock. I can already hear it: the bells ringing in the distance, the caws of gulls growing louder, the layered voices of a waking city stretching toward the ocean. A city full of noise, danger, chaos, and life. A place where I was alone, utterly and completely, the first time I stepped into it, but now I'm different. Now I've stood on a deck slick with blood and made choices I can't undo.

The ship lurches slightly as someone cranks the winch. Another call echoes above deck. "Make ready the lines!" Then I hear a sudden flurry of activity overhead. The crew is moving with purpose, driven by routine, weariness, and the promise of solid ground.

A knock rattles the door. "Sabrina," Isla's voice calls through the wood, muffled but unmistakably excited. "Tomas and I are going to the market! Come with us?"

"I'm coming," I say, though my voice doesn't sound like mine.

I climb the ladder, drawn forward by momentum, noise, and the breathless swell of land drawing closer. I find Isla near the starboard side, her ebony curls pinned up, her sleeves rolled, her face glowing with sweat and anticipation. She wears the pale green dress from Odette's shop, the silk billowing in the wind.

"There she is," Isla says, nodding toward the coastline, and I follow her gaze.

Port Royal sprawls in the distance, bright, brash, familiar in a way that makes my stomach twist. It hasn't changed, but I have.

Gabriel stands at the helm, his hands tight on the wheel, his jaw set as the wind whips his dark hair. He doesn't even look at me.

The moment my feet touch solid ground, it feels like the Earth should stop spinning, but of course it doesn't. Port Royal is already wide awake, the market churning with color and noise and the thick scent of spice and smoke. Isla loops her arm through mine, her energy bright as the morning sun, and Tomas trails behind us, already peeling an orange he must have charmed out of someone's basket.

"First stop, fruit. Second stop, sweets," Isla says, scanning the rows of stalls.

Tomas grins. "That's the spirit."

We weave through the crowd, past baskets overflowing with ginger and guava, crates of salted fish, a caged parrot screeching insults in three languages.

I should be distracted by the chaos, the color, the rhythm of Port Royal, but I can't stop thinking about Gabriel. The look on his face when I couldn't answer him, and the way he didn't look at me as I stepped off the ship.

I try to lose myself in the moment, letting Isla pull me toward a cart where a girl with braids is frying something golden and sticky in a copper pan.

"I'm buying three," Isla says. "No arguments."

Tomas is already handing over a silver coin, winking at the vendor, who nearly fumbles the pan in surprise. We laugh, and for a heartbeat, I forget.

Then I feel a soft roll under my feet, like the ground has taken a long breath beneath us. It's subtle, barely more than a shift, but my heart stops, and I put my hand on my chest, daring not to breathe.

I glance down. The coin Tomas just dropped rolls across the uneven stone, not from his hand, but from the tremor.

"Did you feel that?" I whisper.

Isla frowns. "What?"

"The ground moved."

Tomas kneels to retrieve the coin. "That? Probably just a cannon firing from the harbor. Happens all the time."

But I know better. I know it wasn't a cannon. It was the Earth stirring. My throat goes dry, and the smell of fried sugar turns to ash in my mouth.

It's June 7, 1692. There are only three weeks left. Three weeks until this place is ruined.

I look around at the bustling vendors, the children darting between stalls, the men in wide-brimmed hats shouting about fresh mangos and hot bread, and wonder who among them will survive, who will be crushed, and who will be buried beneath a city that never stood a chance.

Isla's voice cuts through my thoughts. "Sabrina? Are you well?"

I nod quickly, forcing a smile. "Just… dizzy for a second."

Back in our little room, the laughter from the market is already fading like a dream. The window is open to the muggy air, and the sound of gulls bleeds in from the harbor. Tomas tosses a fresh loaf of sweet bread onto the table with a flourish. Isla sinks onto her cot and kicks off her shoes, humming as she unwraps a parcel of still-warm pastries.

I can't eat, and I can't pretend. Instead, I pace, my arms crossed, my heart pounding. The tremor is still in my bones.

Tomas throws himself dramatically onto the floor with a groan. "If we die from overeating, just know I have no regrets."

"We're not dying," Isla says lightly. "We're celebrating a victory, remember? We earned our coin."

"No," I say, louder than I mean to. "We are dying."

They both stare at me. Tomas pushes up on his elbows. Isla sits up straighter. I stop pacing.

"I need to tell you something, and I'm going to sound mad, but I'm not making it up, and I need you to believe me."

They exchange a glance, but it's not the kind that makes me want to backpedal. They're listening.

I take a breath to steady myself. "I'm not from here. Not from this time. I'm from over three hundred years in the future. I was in Port Royal on a historical tour. There was a storm, and I fell into the sea. Eventually, I saw your ship…."

They don't speak; they just stare. I press forward.

"The words you've heard me say that don't make sense to you are words from the future." I drop the British accent that had started to feel natural. "And I'm not part English, part Spanish. I'm American. I'm from New York City. The year is 2025."

Tomas swallows hard, and Isla stares, wide-eyed, at the sudden change in my voice.

"And that tremor, the shaking underfoot at the market, wasn't just cannon fire. It was a warning. In three weeks, on June 7, this city—Port Royal—is going to suffer a massive earthquake. The sea will rush in and swallow most of it. Two-thirds of the city will be gone. Thousands will die."

"How do you know that?" Tomas asks meekly.

"Because it's in the history books," I whisper. "Where I come from, it's already happened. It's one of the most famous disasters in Caribbean history. It was seen as divine punishment for Port Royal's sins."

"That's why you looked like a ghost when the ground shifted," Isla says softly.

I nod. "I've been trying not to say anything. Trying to figure out what to do, but after that tremor… I couldn't stay quiet."

Tomas rubs his hand down his face. "All right. Let's say we believe you, which I think I do because, hell, nothing about you has made sense since the minute we met. What do we do?"

Isla's eyes meet mine, serious now. "How can we warn people?"

"I don't know yet. I don't even know if they'd believe me. I wouldn't have believed me, if I hadn't lived through it."

Isla says quietly, "We need to tell the captain."

My stomach drops. "He was so angry with me this morning."

"He was hurt," she says gently. "You mean something to him, and he can tell you're keeping something from him."

"He called me a liar."

"He was scared," Tomas cuts in. "Men do that, turn fear into anger. Hell, I've done it."

I rub my temples. "What if he doesn't believe me? What if he turns me in to the authorities? What if I ruin everything?"

"What if you save lives?" Isla says, fierce now. "You have a chance to change something, to potentially prevent some of it. If Gabriel knows, he might actually listen."

Tomas nods. "If we're doing this, we do it together."

I sit on the edge of my cot, my heart racing. Three weeks. That's all the time this city has left unless I do something, but what if trying to stop it makes everything worse? What if I change something I was never meant to touch? I could save lives… or I could risk unraveling history itself.

Gabriel's anger cut deeper than I expected. It wasn't just the things he said, but the way he looked at me, like I wasn't who he thought I was. The truth is so much bigger than either of us, and if he couldn't handle my silence, how will he handle the reality? If I tell him everything—about the future, about the earthquake, will it push him even farther away? Or worse, make him wish he'd never let me in at all? The thought of losing him completely makes me feel like I can't breathe, but hiding the truth might destroy us just the same.

DON'T LOOK BACK

GABRIEL

The rum burns on the way down, but I barely taste it. I sit hunched at a corner table in the tavern, the lamplight low, casting gold across the wood. The place stinks of tobacco and brine, and I welcome the sound of laughter, dice clattering, chairs scraping on the floor. It's loud enough to drown out the voice in my head that keeps saying her name.

Sabrina. Damn it all, I hate arguing with her.

It wasn't even a true disagreement. There was no shouting, and she barely said a word. That's what made it worse. I asked for honesty, for something, *anything*—and she looked at me like she wanted to tell me, but then stayed silent. As though I hadn't earned the truth. As though I wasn't worth it.

I slam my mug down, turning a few heads, but no one says anything.

What is she hiding?

There are too many strange things about her–the way she uses words I've never heard, strange and sharp like shards of glass.

I don't want her to tell me everything. I'm not asking for her secrets or her whole bloody soul. Just a sliver, like the place she really comes from. Something to anchor her to the world so I don't feel like I'm falling in love with a ghost.

The rum's hitting harder now, warm and thick behind my ribs. I don't usually drink like this, but I needed something to shut the door between me and her. The door that keeps swinging open in my mind, replaying last night, her mouth on mine, her body under my hands, when she said my name…and now she's gone quiet again.

A tankard thuds down beside my elbow. I glance up, half-expecting a glare, but it's just one of the crew, Cyrus, already turning away with a shrug. "Looked like you needed it," he mutters. I don't remember asking, but I nod all the same. Doesn't matter where it came from. I drink.

I'm not good at being left in the dark. I've spent too long clawing my way out of other people's shadows to let someone I care about cast one over me. She says she's not lying, but withholding the truth feels damn near the same. And the worst part? I'd still choose her. Even if I never get to know why the hell she speaks as though she doesn't belong here. Even if she never tells me where she's truly from.

Leaving the tavern, the streets are slick with evening heat and the scent of something savory roasting in the square. My jaw clenches as I walk fast, and I tell myself I'm just clearing my head, but I know exactly where I'm *really* going.

If Sabrina won't trust me, won't give me so much as a slice of truth, then what am I supposed to do? What kind of future can we possibly have when she meets every question with silence and secrets?

I don't do marriage. Never have. No wife. No woman waiting on some rocky bluff for my return. Just the occasional warmth when I need it, someone who doesn't expect too much. Someone who knows how to read a mood, who can be comforting without strings. Warm, familiar… Annalise.

Her bedroom glows warm from the second floor of the house just off the square, the light spilling soft across the porch. She's a friend who knows how to keep things simple. She's a lover who knows how to keep things wild.

I hesitate at the gate. This isn't where I want to be, not truly, but the ache Sabrina left behind is loud, hollow, and clawing. I need something to drown it, someone who won't look at me like I've broken their heart for asking too much.

Annalise opens the door before I knock. Her auburn hair billows around her face as she tilts her head and leans against the frame. "Well," she says. "Didn't think I'd see you again so soon."

"Wasn't planning to come," I mutter.

"But here you are. I saw you from the window, and my heart began to pound," she says, pulling me inside.

The sitting room is quiet, lit with the glow of a few low lamps. I sink into the armchair by the hearth, rubbing at the back of my neck. She pours two glasses of dark brandy and hands me one.

"Stormy seas, Captain?" she asks lightly.

I drink. "You could say that."

Annalise steps forward, her fingers brushing my arm, then upward, grazing the side of my neck. It's familiar, the way she touches me, slow, certain, like she's mapping skin she already knows. She straddles the ottoman in front of me and leans in, her voice soft in my ear.

"You don't have to say anything," she murmurs. "I know what you need."

That's the truth of the matter; she *does* know. She always has. There's no performance here, no pretending to be someone I'm not. No riddles or secrets wrapped in silk and silence. Just warmth, company, comfort. She leans in, her lips brushing mine, and I let her.

My hands rest on her waist, and that's as far as they go. Her kiss is soft, coaxing, but she's not Sabrina.

I pull back.

"Gabriel?"

"I apologize," I murmur, my voice rough. "I thought this is what I wanted, what I needed."

"You don't have to apologize," she says gently, though I hear the note of disappointment underneath.

"There's a woman…. She makes me feel like I'm losing my mind."

"Then you probably care about her more than you want to."

I look up at her. "She's hiding something. Her words, her habits, the way she looks at the world."

Annalise crosses the room and pours herself another drink. "So why not walk away?"

"I can't. Even with all the secrets, she's the only person who's ever made me want more than survival and a ship to steer, and when she looks at me like she *wants* me, even if she won't let me in, I believe her."

I stand, the room suddenly too small. Annalise doesn't stop me. She walks with me to the door, one hand brushing my arm. "Come back when you know what you need. Or don't. I won't hold it against you."

I nod and hug her goodbye.

The air outside is cooler now, touched with sea breeze and wood smoke. I walk without direction, my hands in my pockets and my heart heavier than when I arrived. I could've buried my feelings tonight. The doubt, the ache, the hurt of being kept at arm's length by someone I want to trust, but I didn't. No matter how far Sabrina pushes me away, I don't want anyone else.

The docks are quieter than usual when I make it back to the ship. Night presses heavy over the harbor, and most of the crew has either wandered off to taverns or collapsed into their bunks. Lantern light sways from the rigging. I climb aboard slowly, my boots echoing in the stillness.

I make it below deck without seeing anyone, but the moment I reach the narrow corridor that leads to the crew quarters, I pause. Her door is slightly ajar, lamplight spilling across the floorboards.

I almost walk by, but at the last second, I knock gently. "Sabrina?"

There's a long pause before she says, "Come in."

She's sitting on the edge of the cot. The oil lamp on the wall burns low, throwing gold across her skin and deepening the shadows under her eyes.

"Good evening," I say, quieter now. "I didn't come to argue. I just... I can't stop thinking about you and what we said. About how it all went to hell this morning." I pause, my heart beating faster. "I don't enjoy disagreeing with you, Sabrina, so I'm trying to understand. Just tell me *something*. Anything. Who you are? What you're afraid of? What you're hiding?"

Her eyes fill with tears, and she blinks fast to keep them from falling. "You wouldn't believe me if I told you."

"Try."

She opens her mouth, then closes it again. For a moment, I think she's going to push me away like before, but then, finally, she speaks.

"There's going to be an earthquake."

I blink. "What?"

She swallows. "Three weeks from now. June seventh. Port Royal is going to collapse into the sea. Thousands of people will die."

My stomach drops. "What are you talking about?"

She rises, her voice shaking now. "I'm not making this up. I *know* it's going to happen."

I stare at her. She's trembling, like just saying it out loud has cracked something inside her.

"Sabrina," I say slowly, "what are you talking about?"

"I can't explain it, not all of it, but you have to believe me. There's not much time. We have to warn people."

I step back a pace. My head is spinning. "You expect me to believe you just *know* the future? That you've seen it?"

Her silence is answer enough.

I shake my head once, sharply. "This is why you've been lying? Keeping secrets? Because you think the world is ending in three weeks?"

"I *know* it is."

A bitter laugh escapes before I can stop it. "You're mad," I mutter. "I knew it. I *knew* there was something off about you."

She flinches. "Gabriel...."

"No," I snap, suddenly cold. "You wouldn't tell me where you're from, why you talk like no one else here, and why you look at Port Royal like it's a ghost."

Sabrina begins to cry.

"And now you expect me to believe you're some kind of prophet, warning us all of Judgment Day?" I laugh again, but there's no humor in it. "I've been a fool. You're just another lost soul with too many stories and nowhere to put them."

"That's not fair," she whispers. "I didn't lie. I just didn't know how to tell you—"

"I don't care," I cut in, sharper than I mean to. "I don't care why anymore. You could've told me *anything*, but you chose this fool's tale."

She takes a step toward me, hand out. "Please—"

"I think you should stay away from me," I say, my voice low and final. "Whatever game you're playing, I want no part of it."

I turn and walk out, the door clicking shut behind me. I don't look back, and I won't.

ST. PETER'S CHURCH

Sabrina

I sit on the edge of the cot, my arms wrapped around myself so tightly it hurts. I'm trying to take deep breaths, but everything inside me feels broken. Tears stream down my face in hot, silent rivers, blurring the lantern light, and soaking into the fabric of the thin blanket pooled in my lap.

When Gabriel was down here, I tried to tell him about the earthquake, and of course he didn't believe me. Isla and Tomas were up on deck then, laughing and playing some game with the crew, but now, they're both back down here in our room, and Gabriel's retreated to his own quarters.

Isla is beside me, her hand resting gently on my back, rubbing slow comforting circles. Tomas sits on the floor in front of us, and neither of them speaks. The only sounds in the small room are the creak of the ship's hull and my own choked sobs.

"I don't—I don't even cry," I say, the words breaking apart in my mouth. "I don't *cry*, not like this, especially not in front of people."

My voice is different now, unmasked. Stripped of the accent I'd carefully adopted to blend in. It's my real voice. New York vowels.

Soft Rs and soft corners. It sounds so foreign in this time, even to my own ears.

"I told him," I whisper, pressing the heels of my hands to my eyes. "I finally told him about the earthquake, and he—he looked at me like I was a lunatic."

Isla draws me into a hug, and I cling to her like I might drown without the anchor of her warmth. She smells of sugar and the spices from the market.

"He doesn't think you're a lunatic," she says quietly. "He's just—confused."

"He said I was mad," I say, laughing bitterly through my tears. "He told me to stay away from him, said he wanted no part of me." My throat tightens. "And maybe he's right. Maybe I never should've said anything. I should've kept my mouth shut and stayed in my place."

"No," Tomas says firmly, crawling forward to put a hand on my knee. "You did the right thing. Even if he doesn't believe you now, he might later. People always doubt the truth when it's too big to swallow."

"I didn't think it would feel like this," I murmur. "I thought telling the truth would be a relief. Like finally coming up for air, but it feels worse. It feels like I lost him."

A knock raps gently at the door, and we all jump. Isla rises to open it. Cyrus stands in the hallway looking uncomfortable, his hat in his hands and his brow furrowed with something between sympathy and guilt.

"Miss Sabrina," he says, clearing his throat. "Captain Ashford's given orders."

My stomach drops. "Orders?"

He nods, his eyes moving briefly to Isla and Tomas before settling on me again. "I've been asking to escort you to St. Paul's church. He said you were to… seek sanctuary there."

I blink at him, stunned. "He's sending me *away*?"

Cyrus shifts uncomfortably. "He said the church would offer protection, food, shelter, and guidance."

Guidance.

"I'm not a danger," I say, more to myself than to him. "I told him the truth."

Cyrus gives a small, awkward nod. "He didn't say otherwise. Just said… it would be best. For everyone."

I stand slowly, my legs unsteady and my heart racing like it wants to shatter through my ribs. "Did he say anything else?"

Cyrus hesitates. Then, quietly adds, "He said to tell you to take care of yourself."

Isla hugs me tightly, whispering something I can barely hear through the ringing in my ears. "I'll come find you tomorrow. We're not letting you go through this alone."

I nod, unable to speak. My throat's too raw, my chest too tight.

As I step out into the hall, following Cyrus toward the gangplank, my heart feels like it's been hollowed out. Gabriel didn't believe me. He didn't fight for me. He just sent me away, and I don't know what's worse—the fear that he's lost to me forever, or the fact that he didn't even look me in the eye when he let me go.

Cyrus's footsteps echo softly on the cobblestones as we leave the ship behind. The harbor's clamor fades with every step, replaced by the hush of narrow streets. My heart pounds as Gabriel's cold dismissal, the impending disaster, and the strange, impossible secret I carry, swirl around inside me.

The streets of Port Royal are quieter now, but they still hum with life, distant laughter, the creak of shutters in the breeze.

I follow Cyrus in silence, the soles of my boots striking stone that feels both real and impossible beneath my feet. I know these streets like the back of my hand from maps, from sketches, and endless late nights in the archives, but walking them now is something else entirely. My heart beats hard with every step, not just because of what's just happened, but because I know what's coming.

We pass Lime Street, and I glance to the left, my pulse catching. That stretch of road will vanish in the quake, pulled under by the sea, but it won't be lost forever. Centuries from now, it'll be discovered beneath the water, almost perfectly preserved. Coins, bottles, the foundations of buildings all frozen in time. A submerged city. An archaeologist's dream, and ahead of us, Chocolata Hole. A calm, dark stretch now, it was once a bay before it was filled in long after the disaster. On the eastern side of that inlet sits St. Peter's Church. I've written papers about this place, but none of that prepared me for the weight of walking into history knowing exactly how and when it ends.

We arrive at a sturdy stone building crowned with a modest steeple, its weathered walls bathed in moonlight. The heavy wooden door creaks open before I can knock, and a man steps out. His face is lined with years of worry and kindness, and his eyes hold a calm I ache to find within myself.

"This is Miss Sabrina." Cyrus's voice is gentle. "Captain Ashford thought she might seek comfort here."

"I'm Reverend Emmanuel Heath. It's wonderful to meet you, Sabrina."

The door closes behind Cyrus with a final thud, muffling the world outside. Inside, the church smells faintly of candle wax and old wood. I follow Reverend Heath toward a quiet corner.

"Please, sit," he gestures to a worn wooden bench. I lower myself cautiously, feeling the cold seep through my dress.

He waits patiently, his hands folded, studying me without judgment. The silence stretches, heavy with everything I want to say but can't quite find the courage to voice.

Finally, I take a shaky breath. "I need to tell you something. Something you may not believe, but it's the truth. I'm not from here, and I'm not from this time." The words taste foreign on my tongue. "I come from the future, over three hundred years ahead. I was visiting Port Royal on a historical tour when a storm swept me away. I woke up here, in 1692."

I watch as his brows knit together, but he doesn't interrupt.

"There's more. In three weeks, on June seventh, this city will be destroyed by an earthquake. The sea will swallow most of it, and thousands will die. I know it will happen—I've read about it. It's history where I'm from."

My voice breaks, but I press on. "I've tried to warn people. I tried to tell Captain Ashford, but he… he doesn't believe me. He thinks I'm mad, that I'm making it up."

I blink back tears, feeling utterly exposed. "Maybe I am crazy. Maybe I'm just a lunatic chasing shadows and stories no one else can see."

Reverend Heath leans forward slightly, his gaze softening. "Miss Sabrina, what you say is extraordinary, and in my years, I have learned not to dismiss the desperate words of a troubled soul. Whether or not your tale is true, you carry a heavy burden."

I nod, feeling utterly defeated. "If you think I'm mad, if you think I need to be locked away for my own good, I understand. I would never hurt anyone, and I don't want to cause a panic, but I can't keep this secret any longer."

He stands slowly, moving to a wooden cabinet, where he retrieves a pitcher of water and a glass. He pours and hands it to me with a gentle smile. "Here. Sometimes, a weary mind needs rest, and a kind heart needs a listening ear."

I take the water gratefully, the coolness soothing my dry throat.

"You are not alone," he says softly. "And if you need shelter, this church will offer you sanctuary."

The thought of safety feels foreign, almost too much to hope for, but beneath it, a fragile flicker of trust begins to grow.

I look up at him, tears threatening again, and manage a small, tired smile. "Thank you, Reverend, for listening."

He nods. "Tomorrow, we will see what can be done. For now, rest, and remember, faith is sometimes found in the most unlikely places."

Reverend Heath leads me down a narrow corridor at the back of the church, his steps quiet on the worn stone floor. He opens a small wooden door. The room is simple but cozy, with a narrow bed, a patchwork quilt, a basin of fresh water, and a small window that lets in the silver haze of moonlight. There's a single candle on the bedside table, its glow soft and warm. "You'll be safe here," he says kindly, then he leaves me in peace.

I sit on the edge of the bed, exhaustion settling into my bones, and for the first time in days, I let my guard down. As I curl beneath the covers, my eyes blur with exhaustion, but before sleep takes me, one thought circles like a storm I can't escape.

How am I ever going to get back to 2025?

TRUST

Gabriel

I can't sleep. The bed creaks beneath me with every shift of my weight, but it's not the swaying that's keeping me up—it's Sabrina.

I stare up at the beams above me, barely visible in the dim lantern light swinging from the wall. The scent of the sea is bitter in the air, mingled with brine and tar. I rub at my sternum like I can dig it out, this dull ache that's been growing since the moment she walked off my ship.

I thought I was protecting her, but perhaps I was protecting myself from her madness. From the part of me that wants her anyway, even when I don't understand anything about her.

I sit up, swing my legs over the edge of the bed, and slide on my boots. The ship is quiet at this hour, most of the crew deep in sleep or still drinking themselves into it. But I know where I'll find the ones who aren't.

Sure enough, when I climb the stairs and slip onto the deck, I find Tomas sitting on a barrel near the bow, his legs pulled up, looking out at the quiet harbor. Isla's beside him, braiding her hair, her eyes fixed on the moonlit water.

They both glance over as I approach. I nod once in greeting, then lean on the railing beside them. No one speaks for a moment.

"She's gone quiet," Isla says finally. "The ship, I mean. Doesn't feel the same without Sabrina."

Tomas nudges a loose rope with his boot. "It was a bit of a brash move, Captain. Sending her off like that."

I exhale sharply through my nose. "Aye."

"She wasn't hurting anyone," Isla says. "Even if she's a little strange. She's a good one. You know that."

"She told me the city was going to fall into the sea," I mutter. "What was I supposed to do with that? Believe her? Start shouting it in the square?"

"No," Tomas says quietly. "But you didn't have to throw her out like she was dangerous."

"I didn't think she was dangerous," I say. "I just didn't know what to do…."

"You could've listened," Isla says, her voice soft but pointed. "Even if you didn't believe her."

"I didn't want to hurt her," I say, more to myself than to them. "I thought she'd lost her mind and needed help I couldn't provide. Perhaps she just trusted me enough to tell the truth, and I threw it back in her face."

Silence again. The wind shifts and carries a hint of rain in from the open sea.

Tomas glances at me. "You know where she is."

"At the church." I nod. "Reverend Heath will take care of her, but it's not where she belongs."

"She belongs here," Isla says, folding her arms. "On this ship. With us."

"With me," I say quietly.

I push off the railing, pacing a few steps. My stomach twists with something too big for words: regret, longing, guilt, all tangled up. I should've followed her. Should've explained. Should've done anything other than send her away like she was some problem I didn't know how to fix.

"I'm going to the church at first light," I say, turning back to face them. "I'll bring her back. If she'll have me."

Tomas nods slowly. "Good."

Isla gives a small smile. "You're not the first man to make a mistake, but if you care about her... don't let pride keep you from making it right."

I nod. "I'll be there as soon as the sun rises."

And this time, I'll listen. Even if it doesn't make sense to me. Even if it scares the hell out of me. I'd rather stand beside a woman with impossible stories and fire in her eyes than live one more day in this world without her.

I'm walking toward the church before the sun's even up, my mind spinning. Sending Sabrina away last night was a mistake I can't take back fast enough. The guilt gnaws at me, sharp and relentless. I need to fix this. I need to find her and make it right.

The wooden door of St. Paul's creaks open. I find Reverend Heath, who leads me to her room.

When I knock, she quietly calls, "Come in."

There she is, sitting on a bed, pale and tired, but all right. The tightness in my chest unravels, the weight I've been carrying finally beginning to lift.

"Sabrina," I say, my voice rough with everything I've held back.

She looks up, her eyes wary but softening when they meet mine.

"I came back for you," I say. "It was terribly wrong of me to send you away. I never should have hurt you this way. Please accept my apology."

"You did what you thought was best, and honestly, speaking with Reverend Heath was incredibly cathartic."

"I want to hear everything you were trying to tell me. I promise I'll listen this time."

She studies me for a long moment, then nods. "Thank you, Gabriel."

We step out into the morning light together, the streets slowly waking. Vendors are setting up stalls, and the smell of fresh bread mingles with wood smoke.

As we walk toward the ship, we cross through the bustling marketplace. I'm so caught up in my guilty thoughts that I almost don't notice the sudden shout.

A woman's voice cracks through the crowd. "Help! My son—he can't breathe!"

I spin toward the sound and spot a small lad, no older than seven or eight, clutching his throat, panic in his eyes. His mother's face is pale with fear, her hands trembling as she tries to help him.

People stop moving, unsure what to do. The boy's breathing is ragged and desperate.

Sabrina doesn't hesitate. She pushes through the gathering crowd and slides her arms around the child's middle from behind.

I barely understand what she's doing until she squeezes upward under his ribs—once, twice—and then a piece of fruit flies free from his mouth. The child gasps in deep, shuddering breaths, collapsing into his mother's arms.

The crowd parts, whispering, stunned. "What was that?" a man asks, his eyes wide.

"That was… strange but it did the job," someone else says in awe.

As the crowd disperses, the mother keeps thanking Sabrina, tears shining in her eyes. Sabrina nods, humble but strong.

I pull Sabrina into a narrow alley, shadows swallowing us from the watchful eyes of the marketplace. My pulse is pounding, part adrenaline, part disbelief.

"How the hell did you know how to do that—to save him?" I demand, my voice low and impatient. "What in heaven was that?"

Sabrina looks at me, her eyes dark and serious, with no hint of fear. Then her usual voice slips away, and something else breaks through, raw, unguarded, and sharper than I've ever heard it. "Gabriel," she says, "I'm not from this time. I'm from the future."

The idea sounds mad, impossible, but the look in her eyes doesn't waver. It's raw and honest, like she's been carrying the weight of keeping this secret from me for too long.

"I know facts you don't," she says. "Information about this city, about the people, about what's coming. I know so many things you can't even imagine."

I stare at her, fighting the urge to laugh or walk away, but something deep inside, something I've felt since the first moment I met her —the mystery, the different way she sees the world—pulls me in closer.

"There's going to be an earthquake," she repeats, her voice urgent this time. "In less than three weeks, Port Royal will be destroyed in an earthquake. The sea will swallow most of the city, and thousands will die. I've read about it in history books from my time."

I swallow hard, the words sinking like stones in my gut.

"We have to warn everyone," she says. "We have to try to save as many people as we can."

I run a hand through my hair, my heart racing. Everything she's said before, everything I doubted, suddenly feels real. She's not crazy or a liar. She's trapped in a nightmare, and she's asking me to believe her.

"Why didn't you tell me this before, that you're from the future?" I ask quietly. "Why hide it?"

"I was terrified," she admits, her voice cracking. "And what is the first thing you did when I tried to tell you about the earthquake? You sent me away. I wish you could trust me."

I reach out and take her hand in mine. "I trust you, Sabrina, and I believe you. We'll figure it out," I say firmly. "Together."

She nods, relief flooding her face. "Thank you, Gabriel."

I pull her into my arms without thinking, holding her like I can shield her from everything. She fits against me like she was always meant to be here. I press a gentle kiss to her forehead. "You don't have to thank me," I murmur. "And I'm not going anywhere ever again."

The noise of the city creeps back in around us, but it fades beneath the burden of Sabrina's words, and the ache in my chest. This isn't just her secret anymore. It's a wound she's letting me tend, and I'll do whatever it takes to prove she can trust me again. The city, the ocean, the earthquake, can wait. Now, all I care about is Sabrina.

FIERCE AND TENDER

SABRINA

Gabriel doesn't run when he hears my authentic voice. He just stares at me like I've set the entire city ablaze, and he's already made peace with the fact that he'd rather stand beside me in the flames than walk away unscathed.

So I start talking about the future. "We don't use ships as much anymore in the twenty-first century. Unless it's for cargo or fun. We fly through the air in massive airplanes that carry hundreds of people. We can cross the ocean in less than a day."

His eyes brim with curiosity and wonder, but I don't give him a chance to ask questions just yet. For the first time in what feels like forever, it feels good to speak freely, to finally share who I am and where I'm from without fear or hesitation.

"In my time, we can talk to people across the world with little boxes in our hands. We can send messages, pictures, and even moving pictures, called videos, with the tap of our fingertips. It's possible to have entire conversations just through those little boxes. We've been among the stars. We've even sent people up to walk on the moon."

"The moon?" he echoes, as though trying to be certain he heard me right.

I nod. "People have set foot on the moon in my time."

Gabriel lets out a low exhale, a sound that falls somewhere between reverence and disbelief. "This sounds like a myth or a fairy tale."

I smirk. "You sound like a man who needs coffee."

"Coffee I know," he says dryly. "We're not completely uncivilized."

We begin walking again, heading toward the quieter edge of the city. The tension between us has shifted. Gabriel is no longer suspicious but instead filled with curiosity. It feels like he's truly seeing me now.

"So how does your world run without sails?" he asks. "Is it all flying machines and talking boxes?"

"More or less. We have what we call cars, fast metal carriages that are powered by engines instead of using horses. We often travel by roads called highways, and they stretch across entire countries. Some of the bigger cities have subway trains, which are like many cars strung together that go so fast you feel your bones vibrate."

"And what do you do, in your time?" His tone is casual, but I catch the note of interest beneath it. He wants to know me, not just my world.

"I was a museum archivist," I say. "I studied places like this and people like—well, like you."

He stops walking. "You studied about me?"

I giggle. "Not you specifically, but your century and the people who live here now. Colonial life in the Caribbean. The slave trade. Imperialism. All the parts that your world tries to keep tidy and respectable."

Gabriel's expression darkens, though not at me. "You don't soften it."

"Why would I? History's already been cleaned up too many times. My job was to help people see the real stories behind the names and dates. The mess, the cost, the fight, as well as the love."

He studies me closely. "No wonder you don't scare easily."

"I'm here now, and I don't know how long I've got or if I'll ever make it back, but I'm not going to play dumb and pretend I don't know what's coming. I've seen the death toll from this earthquake. I've read the survivor accounts, the casualty lists, and I can't just watch this happen without trying to help."

Gabriel is quiet for a moment, then says, "We will need to think of a way to get as many of the women and children out of the city as we can. In the meantime, tell me what you miss the most. What are you homesick for?"

"I miss my city, even the honking horns, the subway heat, and greasy pizza at two in the morning. I miss air conditioning and hot showers, but most of all, I miss my best friend, Maddie."

His gaze softens. "Your sister?"

I glance up at him. "She was like a sister. We grew up together."

"I'm sorry, Sabrina. It must be difficult not knowing what happened on her side."

We walk for a time, arm in arm. His body is relaxed, but I can feel the quiet tension just beneath the surface in the slight twitch of his fingers, the way his gaze flicks toward me and then away. I know that look, that quiet hum of curiosity just behind his eyes. I can practically hear the gears turning in his mind as he sorts through everything I've told him, weighing it, wondering what to ask next.

The scents of smoke, bread, and sea salt surround us as we slip inside the tavern. It's quieter than usual, with only a few men seated at a far table and a yawning barmaid sweeping the floor. We sit at a small wooden table, tucked beneath a low window. Gabriel orders for us, and soon a steaming mug is set in front of me, dark and fragrant.

I take a sip, bracing for the usual bitter slap I've been drinking on the ship, and then pause.

He notices. "What?"

"This is... really good," I say, blinking down at the mug. "Like, better-than-the-future good."

His brow arches, amused. "Better than your twenty—?"

"Twenty twenty-five," I say, smiling. "And yes. In my time, coffee's fast and over-processed. This—this tastes like someone actually cared when they made it."

Gabriel chuckles, watching me take another sip, slower this time. "We may not have much, but we do take our coffee seriously."

I glance up and catch the way he's studying me again, not with doubt or suspicion, but with wonder.

"So," Gabriel says, his eyes fixed on me like I'm a riddle just beginning to unravel, "you're from a place called New York City?"

I smile. "Yes, but in your time, it isn't called that yet. You'd know it as New Amsterdam."

He tilts his head, his brow furrowed. "That's Dutch territory, near the Hudson River, is it not?"

"It was," I nod. "The Dutch founded it in the early 1600s, but in 1664, the English took it over and renamed it New York. In my time, it's one of the largest cities in the world."

He lets out a quiet whistle, leaning back in the wooden chair. "From a trading post to one of the largest cities in the world. That's hard to imagine."

"It's almost impossible to describe," I admit. "There are more people living there now than in all the colonies combined. The streets stretch for miles, crowded with every language you can think of, and some of the buildings are so tall, they disappear into the clouds."

He raises an eyebrow. "Taller than a ship's mast?"

I laugh softly. "Try a hundred masts stacked one on top of the other."

His expression shifts between awe and disbelief. "How does a building stand that tall?"

"Steel," I explain. "We've made it stronger than anything. In my time, we use it to build towers, bridges, and even machines."

Gabriel shakes his head slowly, clearly trying to picture it all. "And these people... they live in the sky?"

"In a way," I say. "We live high up, work in offices, study in libraries bigger than cathedrals, and there are moving carriages powered by engines, not horses. Roads made of stone and something called asphalt, smooth enough to glide across. It's noisy, crowded, chaotic... but it's home."

He stares into his mug for a moment, then asks, "How do you know all this about New Amsterdam? About what it becomes?"

I smile, touched by his question. "Because I live it through the artifacts in the museum. I study old maps, journals, records, and artifacts from people just like you. I've seen maps from your time, even letters from settlers who lived in New Amsterdam. I've read about the port, the trade, the conflicts. I've held those pieces of the past in my hands."

His eyes narrow with interest. "So… in your world, my time is the past, and you've read about it in these artifacts?"

"Exactly," I say. "I've spent my whole life preserving stories like yours. I never thought I'd end up living one."

Gabriel lets the thought settle before he speaks again. "It's strange, is it not? I've always looked ahead, trying to see what lies beyond the next tide or storm; here you are, looking backward, and somehow, we meet in the middle."

"We're both chasing something," I murmur. "Maybe we're not so different after all."

A quiet smile touches his lips. "Perhaps not."

And for a little while, we just sit there together, two people from different centuries, sharing the same coffee, the same table, and the same quiet peace between stories.

After coffee and breakfast, Gabriel guides me through the bustling streets of Port Royal. The market hums with life. People haggle with vendors, fabrics flutter like ribbons, and the rich aroma of spices carries in the air. I walk beside him, taking in the rough beauty of the town: wooden buildings leaning into one another, rickety carts bouncing over uneven stones, smoke curling from chimney tops, and the ever-present thrum of people moving, shouting, bartering.

As we walk, he speaks of the town's growth, how it thrives despite the constant dangers from the sea and the thick jungle beyond.

I listen closely, drawn in by his voice and by the strange, precarious world he calls home. It feels so far from the one I left behind, and yet beneath the grit and noise, I recognize something universal–hope, fear, ambition, and the hunger to carve out a life in the middle of chaos.

As the sun climbs higher, we drift toward the waterfront. The harbor opens wide before us, scattered with ships flying flags from every corner of the world–English brigs, Dutch sloops, and Spanish galleons. Gabriel shares tales of sailors and merchants, of pirates and privateers who prowl the Caribbean in search of fortune or vengeance.

We settle on a weathered dock, our feet swinging just above the water. I lean into him, the steady warmth of his arm a quiet reassurance. Around us, the day carries on. Ropes creak, men shout from the decks, and seagulls circle overhead.

The afternoon slips by in slow golden strokes, and eventually, we make our way back toward the tavern. Inside, the usual noise fades into the background as we share a simple meal of salted pork, potatoes, bread, and mugs of dark, rich brandy. There's a kind of peace in the quiet between us.

By the time we step outside, the sky is a canvas of deep amber and rose, the last light of day. The heat has broken, replaced by a breeze that feels like a promise of rest.

Gabriel reaches for my hand, and he wraps his fingers around mine. "Walk home with me," he says, and I do.

The stars are already climbing into the sky when we reach the dock. I feel Gabriel's thumb brush over my knuckles as we walk side by side.

When we meet the edge of the water, the longboat is waiting, bobbing gently against the post. Gabriel helps me in first, his hand firm around mine, and then climbs in after me. The oars dip into the sea with a quiet rhythm, and we drift back toward the ship under the moonlight. I sit close to him, our shoulders pressed together, my skirt brushing his knee. The world is hushed and silver, and I can feel the warmth of his gaze even when I am not looking at him.

He ties the boat with practiced ease when we arrive and helps me onto the deck with a touch that lingers longer than it needs to. The crew is quiet tonight, scattered or already asleep. Lanterns swing low on the rigging, casting pools of light across the worn wood. He leads me below deck, each step slower than the last, like neither of us is quite ready to break the silence. We keep walking until we reach his quarters.

Inside, the cabin is still and dim, the only light coming from the small lantern on the wall. The bed looks freshly made, the sheets tucked with neat precision, though the pillow has the shape of someone who sleeps restlessly. I stand in the center of the room for a moment, listening to the creak of the ship around us, the water slapping gently against the hull.

Gabriel watches me from just inside the door, his expression unreadable, but his eyes are steady. I turn to face him, my heart beating a little faster now.

I reach for him first, sliding my fingers along the collar of his shirt, and he exhales slowly, like he's been holding his breath. He steps forward, closing the space between us, and cups my face in his hands. When his lips touch mine, it is slow and certain. I melt into him, my arms winding around his neck, my body pressed against the solid line of his. The kiss deepens, his hand slipping to my waist.

We move together without speaking, like we've done this before in another life. He lifts me gently, setting me down on the edge of the bed, then kneels to remove my boots. When he leans in again, his lips skim the hollow of my throat, and I shiver at the tenderness in his touch.

Clothes fall away slowly, quietly, like a secret unfolding. His skin is warm against mine, and I trace the shape of his shoulder, the scar near his ribs, the curve of his back. There's something raw in his gentleness, like he's afraid I'll vanish if he holds me too tightly. I guide him closer, grounding him with my body, and with the press of my mouth against his jaw. We don't rush. There is time to explore in this moment, time to learn each other's bodies.

I reach for his hand, guiding him closer until he stands just in front of me, his eyes searching mine. My voice is quiet as I look up at him and say, "Lie down on the bed." There's no demand in it, only an invitation, something soft and vulnerable between us.

He settles back onto the bed, his eyes never leaving mine. I climb over him, guiding us together with a slow, deliberate grace. The look that crosses his face–part wonder, part surrender–is one I'll remember for the rest of my life.

I grind on his cock slowly at first, savoring the way he fills me, his hands grip my hips, steadying me. But the need builds quickly, hot, insistent, and I move faster, chasing the rhythm that makes his eyes darken with hunger. His hands slide up my sides, callused fingers trailing fire across my skin, until his mouth finds my breast. The warmth of him there nearly undoes me. He sucks gently, then harder, in time with the rising pace of my hips.

Our bodies find harmony as I ride him harder, faster, until there's nothing left between us but heat, and the wild rush of sensation. He groans against my skin, one hand tangled in my hair, the other clutching my thigh as if letting go would break him. I'm close—so close—and when I look down into his eyes, blazing with need and something more tender, it tips me over.

I cry out his name as I come, and he follows with a groan, his body tensing beneath mine as we fall over the edge together.

Afterward, I lie tangled in the warmth of Gabriel's arms, his steady breath against my skin, and for the first time in what feels like forever, the weight of all the secrets and the impossible truths between us seems lighter. Now, he believes me, *truly* believes me, and that faith is stitching together the frayed edges of my trust piece by piece.

Even if I have nothing else, even if I am lost in a century that was never meant for me, at least I am here with a man who makes love like a god, fierce and tender all at once.

HISPANIOLA

Gabriel

Sabrina and I lie awake, and what she shared echoes in my mind. Port Royal is fragile, temporary, a castle built on shifting sand, and we are caught in its slow collapse.

I trace the curve of her jaw in the dim light, memorizing the contours of a woman who carries burdens I barely understand. Her strength is fierce, but I see the worry beneath. She carries fears for this city and the future, and an ache of a secret too heavy for one to hold alone.

"We have to do something," I whisper, my voice rough with exhaustion. "But we can't just warn the city outright. They won't listen, or worse, they'll panic, and we'll be arrested for starting a riot."

She nods, her eyes still closed. "I've been thinking about that. There's another way, something to draw people away."

"Like what?" I ask, leaning closer.

Sabrina sighs softly. "Greed. The lure of treasure. If we plant rumors of a hidden Spanish cache just outside the city, riches forgotten during the wars, people will leave in droves to seek it. It's not noble. It's desperate, but it might save lives."

I smirk, knowing all too well the poison and power of greed in this town. Men like me, used to chasing fortune and fighting for scraps, know exactly how to use that. "You want me to spread whispers in the taverns, and on the docks, make sure the right ears catch the rumors?"

"Exactly," she says. "You know the streets better than I ever will. You know who spreads gossip."

I brush a stray curl from her face. "We'll send them inland, to St. Jago de la Vega. It's safer there, solid ground, farther from the sea."

"Spanish Town, right?" she asks.

"Aye. That's what some call it now. I'll do it, then. I'll stir the pot, but we have to be careful."

"Whatever I can do to help, I will. I can use what I know to keep us one step ahead." Sabrina curls against me as I run my fingers slowly through her hair. "We wait," she whispers. "Two or three days before it happens—that's when we warn the city."

My arm tightens around her. "Whatever gets them moving. Whatever saves the most people."

We lie tangled together in the quiet dark, the ship rocking gently beneath us, her head resting on my chest, and though I try to stay awake, to savor the nearness of her, the warmth of her body, I drift into sleep, the magnitude of her re-earned trust wrapped around me like a promise.

* * *

Dawn breaks warm and bright. I blink awake slowly, my arm still draped around Sabrina. For a long moment, I just lie there, breathing her in, feeling her body against me. How oddly natural, like no matter what century she came from, she was always meant to find her way into my bed, my world, and my life.

She stirs, stretching with a quiet sigh. Her eyes open, hazy with sleep, but focused when they land on me.

Over a meager breakfast of oranges and weak coffee, I begin to form a plan. "We need to get them out," I say softly. "At least the main crew."

Sabrina props herself up on one elbow. "Then let's take them away from the city. Hispaniola. They won't question a trip there. Not if you say it's for trade or new opportunities."

"Aye," I murmur, already turning the idea over in my mind. "It's far enough to keep them safe, and close enough to return after."

She reaches for my hand. "We don't have to lie. Just… leave out the reason. Say we're sailing there for something important. All you'd have to do is give them the orders and get them aboard."

"We'll say it's to scout out new waters. New alliances. Perhaps even a rumored cache left behind in the hills. They won't need much convincing."

"They trust you," Sabrina says, rising and reaching for her shift. "And if they don't… they follow you anyway."

I dress quickly, buckle my belt, and slide my knife into place. Sabrina dresses and braids her hair back, her expression focused.

On deck, the air smells of brine and sun-warmed wood. The crew's already stirring, Isla's cooking in the galley, and Tomas is inspecting a torn sail. Cyrus sharpens a blade with the edge of a whetstone, all familiar things, and none of them know how close they are to the edge.

I gather them near the helm just after breakfast, casual but firm. "We make for Hispaniola," I announce. "There's business there, potential allies, and opportunities worth exploring. We won't be long, but I want full sails ready by midday."

No one questions me, and by midmorning, we're hauling anchor and catching the wind. The sails snap to life above us, the ship turning toward open sea with a groan and a surge. The shoreline of Port Royal begins to drift behind us, shrinking slowly as the waters widen ahead.

I stay at the wheel, my hands firm and ready. The men cheer as we hit a smooth current, already talking of new coins, beautiful women, and strong rum.

Sabrina stands with Isla, Tomas, and Cyrus—four sharp-eyed souls I'm trusting with the ship's fate when the time comes.

I instruct the main crew to watch from the side, and offer advice or step in to demonstrate when needed, but the five of us will sail back without them, so now is the time to learn. It's a slow lesson in patience and precision, one that can't be rushed.

"All right," I call out, my voice cutting through the bustle. "Cyrus, hold the wheel steady. This isn't just about strength. It's feel, anticipation. Read the water and the wind."

He grips the wheel tighter, his eyes fixed ahead as a ripple rolls beneath the hull.

Isla steps forward, looping a line around the belaying pin with careful fingers. "This way?" she asks, glancing toward one of the older sailors, who nods approvingly.

"Good," I say. "Now, Tomas, next you'll help Isla with the foresail. You'll need to haul it up without snapping the sheets."

Tomas grunts but moves with determination, his muscles flexing as he pulls. One of the veteran crew members claps him on the back. "Steady now. Think rhythm, not brute force."

Sabrina watches closely, absorbing every move. When it's her turn, I hand her a coil of rope. "Trim the mainsail, keep it tight when I give the word. The better you are at this, the faster we'll move. Again," I say firmly. "This time, tighter, quicker. The ocean won't wait for us to catch up."

We run through the drills, the sails rising and falling in sync with shouted commands, the lines snapping taut then slackening. Mistakes come fast, but corrections come faster. The main crew steps in without hesitation, offering tips, adjusting grips, steadying nerves.

Hours pass, the sun dips low, sweat drips, and lungs burn, but the rhythm solidifies. The skeleton crew moves with growing confidence, their bodies syncing with the ship's pulse.

When I finally call an end, one of the older sailors claps Tomas on the shoulder. "You've got the heart of a true sailor, lad."

Tomas grins, wiping sweat from his brow. "Feels good to finally get it right."

I take a slow breath, feeling the pressure of what's ahead–leaving the main crew safe on solid ground in Hispaniola, sailing away from them, and knowing the risk and the distance that stretches between us.

My focus narrows to Sabrina, Isla, Tomas, and Cyrus, the few I trust to hold the ship and navigate the dangers ahead. Every decision from here on out is for their safety, and for Sabrina. Without her, nothing else means a damn thing.

THE CHOICE IS CLOSE NOW

Sabrina

Four days later.

"Land ho!"

The call rings out, and Gabriel joins me at the railing as the island comes into view, lush and jagged on the horizon, the sea around it deep blue.

"Hispaniola," he says quietly. "Graceful name for a place so fierce."

I nod. "It stays fierce. In my time, it's two countries—Haiti on the west, the Dominican Republic on the east."

He glances at me. "Still split?"

"Yes, it's complicated. Haiti's born out of a revolution, the only successful uprising of enslaved people in history. They take their freedom and name their country themselves. The Dominican side fights its own battles for independence. Neither path is easy. This island has been carved up, fought over, and bled on for generations, but it endures."

He nods slowly, his gaze shifting back to the land. "Then it makes sense that we brought the crew to a place that knows how to survive. We'll anchor near the southern coast," he says, "far from prying eyes."

The crew bustles around us, hauling rope, lowering sails, and shouting instructions. They still don't know exactly why we've come, only that Gabriel said it was important, and that it was safer than the city.

By evening, we make it ashore, the longboats cutting through shallows and sand. We set up camp just inland, tucked between leaning palms and tall grasses.

A breeze moves through the trees, and in the goosebumps on my skin, and the way it feels like the island is watching us, I can tell Hispaniola is wild and untamed in a spiritual way.

We sit behind a patch of scrubby bushes near the edge of the camp. Tomas is sprawled in the dirt nearby, drawing in the sand with a stick. Isla perches on a fallen log, braiding ribbons into her hair while chewing on a slice of mango.

The fire crackles low, throwing flickers of orange and gold across the clearing as the night deepens around us. The voices that once filled the space have softened, first to murmurs, then to silence.

One by one, the crew drifts off, offering tired nods and quiet goodnights as they retreat to their tents or roll up in blankets under the stars. Tomas goes first, yawning mid-sentence, and then Isla falls asleep too. Even the laughter fades, leaving only the pop of embers and the low hum of insects in the jungle beyond.

Gabriel and I share a tent, which is little more than canvas and rope, pitched beneath the thick canopy of trees not far from the coast. It holds in the warmth of Gabriel's body beside mine. He's already asleep, his arm draped over my waist.

Outside, the birds trill in a thousand different songs. Leaves rustle, and not far off, something growls low and deep before falling silent again. I lie still, listening to every sound of the jungle, every nuance a reminder that I am very far from everything I once called home.

Gabriel shifts in his sleep, pulling me closer. His cheek brushes my arm. I close my eyes and breathe him in. He makes me feel safe, even now, even here.

The earth under the thin bedroll is uneven, knotted with roots. The heat sticks to my skin, and still, I don't want to be anywhere else. Not without him.

Above us, the trees share secrets in a language older than either of us. This island feels ancient in a way I can't explain. It seems to remember everything–every rebellion, past, present, or future. Every storm, every battle, every sacrifice made in its name.

I press my hand over Gabriel's where it rests against my stomach and whisper into the dark, "We're not alone here."

I sense more than the animals and the nearby villagers. Spirits, Mother Nature, goddesses of the wind… if Earth remembers, I hope she remembers mercy.

* * *

The week unfolds like a storybook I never thought I'd step into, each day a page drenched in color, scent, and sound. Hispaniola spreads before us, a gorgeous beast, alive with life beneath its sweltering sun. I'm trained to look, to catalog, to piece together fragments of the past, but here, it's different. I'm not just observing history, I'm living it.

We wander through dense thickets where towering ceiba trees stretch their ancient arms toward the sky, their bark scarred with the marks of time and human hands. The forest is dense and smells of damp earth, wild orchids, and salt water carried from the nearby sea. Brightly colored birds dart through the cover, their calls sharp and piercing, weaving with the chatter of monkeys hidden just out of sight.

In the villages we pass, wooden huts with thatched roofs huddle together, smoke billowing from their stone hearths. Children with bare feet chase chickens, their laughter ringing down the dirt paths. Women in vibrantly hand-dyed skirts carry baskets heavy with plantains and cacao pods, and Heaven help me, the scent of roasting coffee drifts from open windows, mingling with the spicy sweetness of freshly ground nutmeg.

Everywhere I look, there are stories etched into the land, tales of the island's Taíno ancestors. Fields of sugarcane bend in the breeze, cruel promises of wealth born of suffering.

The thick jungle parts like a curtain of green as we approach a clearing, and I gasp at the sight before me: ancient stone carvings swallowed by vines, their curves worn but still proud.

I turn to Gabriel. "These are Taíno petroglyphs, etched deep into the rock."

I step closer, tracing the faded spirals and faces with my eyes, imagining the tales they held of gods, nature, and life before the world changed.

Gabriel squints at the carved wooden figure nestled among the artifacts. "Who were these people? The ones who made these?"

"The Taíno people were the original inhabitants of these islands—Hispaniola, Puerto Rico, Cuba, and others. They lived here long before Europeans arrived."

He shifts closer, intrigued. "I've heard stories, but I don't know much. What happened to them?"

"The Taíno suffered from diseases brought by the Europeans, like smallpox, and from brutal forced labor and warfare. Their population dropped dramatically in just a few decades. It's a tragic story."

Gabriel's gaze darkens. "This island is more than just land or treasure. It holds the memories of a people nearly lost."

I nod. "Exactly. Their culture, their art–they left traces of who they were, and it's important we remember them, especially here."

Nearby, a cluster of ceremonial zemis, sacred sculptures of wood and stone, sit gathered on a low altar, their shapes mysterious and haunting. My fingers itch to touch them, but I hold back, knowing their significance is more than just history; they are the pulse of a people erased but never silenced. This land is layered with soul, tragedy, love, war, pain, happiness, and for a moment, I feel like I'm not a stranger here, but a witness to an ancient legacy that still breathes.

* * *

One morning as the sun rises high, setting the sky ablaze with streaks of orange and pink, Gabriel tells me he needs to head into the nearby settlement to gather supplies.

"We need food, rope, and other supplies for the journey ahead." He gives Isla and Tomas a sharp look, like they're the ones he's trusting to keep me safe while he's gone.

I watch him disappear down the narrow path, his broad shoulders blending into the shadows of the jungle. The air grows thick and humid, the sounds of unseen creatures humming all around us. Isla braids flowers into her curls, stealing quick glances at me, while Tomas pokes at a cluster of ants with a curious finger.

Finally, Isla breaks the silence. "We want to take you somewhere."

Tomas nods, his eyes dark and serious. "To meet someone."

I'm intrigued. "Who did you have in mind?"

Isla grins, a mischievous sparkle in her eyes. "She lives past the cane fields, near the old sacred grove. People say she's mad, but when you've got a problem that rum can't fix, she's the one you seek."

"She might be able to help you with your peculiar 'being-from-the-future predicament,' Tomas adds. "Perhaps the witch can send you back. That is, if you even want to go back home."

I giggle. "You actually believe she can help?"

Tomas shrugs. "I believe it's worth a try."

I stare at the cracked dirt beneath us, the wild island around us still buzzing with life. "If she really could send me back... that would mean surviving this. That would mean not dying in Port Royal."

Isla leans forward earnestly. "What have you got to lose by simply meeting her? And if it means you can go back home before the earthquake hits, it will be worth it. We hate to see you go, but we want you to be safe."

A flicker of hope blooms in my chest, wild and fragile. I've spent weeks bracing for the end—working to change fate for others, never daring to think I'd find a way out for myself.

Now, here they are, offering me a path I never imagined. "Let's find your witch."

Tomas grins, and Isla stands, brushing the dust off her skirt. "Come on. It's a long walk, and she doesn't take visitors after sunset."

We slip away quietly, the island's lush woods swallowing us whole. Tomas leads us down a rugged path. My skirts catch on thorns, but I push forward. I need to know if there's a way back home.

At last, we reach a crooked, weathered hut leaning deep into the greenery, nearly swallowed by moss and creeping vines. A circle of tiny bones clacks softly above the door in the humid breeze.

Tomas knocks once, and the door creaks open. An old woman stands on the threshold, her skin rough like tree bark, her eyes gleaming amber like hardened sap. Beads and bones tangle at her throat, and her thick gray hair is wrapped tightly in a beautiful indigo wrap. She doesn't frown or smile.

"You brought the one with the storms in her blood," she says.

I freeze. "I beg your pardon?"

She turns, beckoning us inside. Tomas nudges me forward. "That means you."

Inside, bottles line the shelves, filled with floating things I don't want to name. The floor is painted with strange symbols. In the corner on the floor, something stirs in a cage, but I dare not look.

The witch settles at a table, and without invitation, we sit too.

"You're not from here," she says, eyes locking on mine. "You've seen steel towers. Light without flame. Roads like rivers."

"Yes," I admit. "I'm from the year 2025."

She leans forward suddenly, grabbing a shallow bowl carved from dark stone from the table. She sets it between us and pours in a murky liquid from a cracked flask.

Next, she pulls a handful of dried herbs and crushed shells from a pouch at her side and lets them fall into the mix. The surface ripples once, twice, then becomes still. She stares into it without blinking, the fire casting her reflection in a thousand fractured shapes. Her breath grows slow.

"Mmm," she hums, her eyes locked on the water. "The sea brings you from far away and long from now." The liquid starts to swirl and steam. "Glass towers, a road striped in white, a carriage that moves without horses. I see the storm that carried you. I see the tear that waits to open again." She blinks once and looks up at me. "The choice is close now."

She speaks low, her voice like smoke. "When the Earth breaks open, the sea will come. Water, wind, sky and time will tear, all at once. A door will open where no door should be. You were pulled through by the storm. The storm will take you back."

My blood runs cold.

"Only if you are willing to stay. The storm does not steal—it serves. You must choose. Stay or go."

I glance at Tomas and Isla, who are both pale and silent.

I think of Gabriel, the way his hand finds mine without hesitation. The way he kisses me like I belong here.

I think of Port Royal, and of the destruction I know is coming—the death and ruin.

"You're sure?" I ask. "This… this really could take me home?"

The witch nods. "The storm will come with the wave. Be ready. You will feel it in your bones. You will know."

Silence presses in. No trinkets. No spell. Just truth, laid bare and quiet.

Behind me, Tomas shifts uncomfortably, and Isla doesn't move at all. Finally, Tomas clears his throat. "We should return to camp."

I nod slowly, my legs stiff as I rise. The hut suddenly feels too small.

We walk back in silence. Each step away from that crooked hut feels heavier than the last, like the ground knows what I haven't yet admitted aloud. The quake is coming, and when the sea rises, it may take this world, or send me back to mine, but for the first time since I fell through time, the choice is in my hands.

Stay, and risk everything for love and a life not meant for me… or leave, and carry this wild, broken beauty only in memory.

SPANISH COLORS

I push aside the fronds, ducking under a low branch as Cyrus and I break through the last stretch of jungle toward camp. The sun is high now, and sweat trickles down my neck, soaked into the collar of my shirt. My pack is loaded down with fresh rope, dried meat, and a few tools we bartered from a fisherman near the inlet. I hear familiar voices ahead and pick up my pace.

When we arrive at camp, the first faces I see are Tomas, then Isla, clutching her skirt with one hand and a bundle of wild herbs in the other. Sabrina walks behind them, quiet, her face unreadable until she spots me and smiles.

After walking toward me and wrapping me in a tight embrace, she says, "We went to see a witch."

I glance between her and the others. "*A witch?*"

"More like a Voodoo priestess," she says, and for a moment I think she's jesting, "She lives in an old grove. Tomas and Isla brought me to see her."

Cyrus makes a noise in his throat behind me, but I ignore him. "And what exactly did she tell you?"

Sabrina glances toward the campfire where someone's already

started laying out food. She doesn't answer right away, just nods toward the flames. "Come sit. I'll explain."

We gather around the fire, plates passed between us, charred fish and boiled plantains. Sabrina picks at hers without eating. "The witch said I can go home," she says finally, her voice hushed. "Back to twenty twenty-five. When the earthquake comes, when the tsunami hits Port Royal, she said that storm is my doorway."

I set my plate down, not because I'm done eating but because my appetite vanishes with her words. "How?"

"She said the same type of storm that brought me here could send me home. When the sea comes, the wind, the sky tearing open—it'll happen again, and if I'm ready, if I stay in Port Royal, it might return me to my time."

Her voice wavers at the end, and my chest aches at the thought. "Do you want that?" I ask, carefully, quietly. "To go home?"

She meets my eyes, and it feels like everything slows for a beat. "I don't know," she says. "I mean, I want to see Maddie and my family again. My friends and colleagues. I want to wake up in a world that makes sense to me, do my job, live my old life... but then I look at you, and I don't want to leave."

I shift closer, taking her hand, and she doesn't pull away. "You don't have to decide today," I say, even though the storm is already on its way. "Although, we both know we can't stay here much longer."

She nods. "We need to return to Port Royal and try our plan–the taverns, the gossip. We can scare people off and give them enough warning."

"We'll need every hour," I say. "We'll leave tomorrow to warn Port Royal."

She leans against my shoulder, and I feel the gravity of her decision pressing on us both. "I'll miss you too much," she whispers.

I swallow hard. "Then stay."

Her silence is louder than any answer.

* * *

The sun's just starting to dip behind the trees, the sky streaked with orange and violet when I call the crew together. Most of them are sprawled around camp, oiling blades, checking packs, sharing the last of the boiled plantains. They rise slowly, one by one, wiping sweat from their brows, and tightening their boots.

I step onto the flattest patch of ground near the fire, my hands at my sides, my heart thudding. Sabrina stands a few paces behind me, and Tomas and Isla sit beside her. Cyrus lingers near the edge of the circle, his arms crossed, already knowing what I'm about to say.

"Lend me your ears," I begin, loud enough to cut through the low drone of insects. "We've a new course."

That earns a few mutters, heads tilting, brows furrowing. I wait until every eye is on me.

"Tomorrow morning," I say, "I'm returning to Port Royal, and I'm only taking Sabrina, Tomas, Isla, and Cyrus with me. The rest of you stay here."

The murmurs swell, but I raise a hand before anyone can speak. "You'll be safe here. We've built a fine camp. You've got supplies, and each of you will be paid now, in gold." I reach into the sack at my feet, pulling out a heavy pouch. I toss it to the nearest man, and he catches it with both hands and opens it. The weight and shimmer of it shuts him right up.

"I'll return for you. Two weeks, maybe four at the most. Trust me."

"Why are you leaving us, Cap'n? Why not take the whole crew?"

"Our next battle is in Port Royal, and it isn't your fight," I say without flinching. "There's danger in the city, and you're not risking your lives when it's not your burden to carry."

That hangs heavy in the air, but no one protests, not with gold in their hands. They glance at one another, uneasy perhaps, but not angry. They trust me, and trust I'll keep my word.

"Stay close to camp," I tell them. "Don't stir trouble with the locals. Don't talk about what we're doing here, and when I come back, we sail for the open sea for more coin than you've ever dreamed."

Someone gives a high-pitched whistle. Another shouts a sharp, "Aye, Captain."

That's all I need, and I feel the pride of leadership settle into my bones.

The camp quiets as night deepens, the jungle humming in the hush between firelight and sleep. We don't speak much after the meeting, just the sounds of boots scuffing dirt, a few shared nods, the low murmur of men settling into sleep.

Sabrina lies beside me in the tent, her body pressed against mine. I keep one arm around her, her heartbeat steady beneath my hand.

She doesn't fall asleep quickly, and neither do I.

"Are you still considering your options?" I whisper.

She nods. "My mind is bouncing between my choices and the storm."

I press a kiss to her forehead. "We'll face it all together."

Eventually, her breathing evens. I lie awake a little longer, listening to distant birds and the occasional snap of twigs. The sky is thick with stars, and I count them until I drift off.

* * *

Dawn breaks hot and quick. We're up before the sun fully crests the treetops. The crew stirs into motion, gathering supplies, rolling up tents, lashing barrels shut.

The longboats are already waiting at the shore, bobbing gently where we left them. Sabrina double-checks the wrapped bundles of maps and food. I watch her tuck a borrowed compass into her belt, her brow furrowed with focus.

I nod to Tomas. "Let's move."

We load the boats quickly, the main crew helping with practiced hands, quiet and respectful. The tide's with us. I can feel it in my gut. One push and we'll be at sea.

The sky is still streaked with gray when the watchman's cry rips through the morning. "Ship on the horizon! Flying Spanish colors— she's bearing straight for us!"

The ship drifts in closer than any friendly vessel ought to. I watch from the shallows where the longboats are nearly loaded, my hands tightening at my sides. The crew, what little we can see of them, move with too much purpose. I hear no laughter or chatter aboard, only quiet figures in formation.

Then, before anyone can speak, a sharp crack splits the morning.

A musket shot. The ball strikes the sand at our feet, kicking up dust. Another follows, closer. Instinct takes over. "Down!" I shout, drawing my pistol as I drop behind a barrel.

All around me, the camp erupts into motion. Isla screams. Tomas scrambles for cover. The enemy reaches shore, returning fire. So much for a peaceful departure. Whoever these lads are, they didn't come to trade.

I whirl around to face my crew. "To arms!" I bellow.

Cyrus tosses an extra musket toward me. I catch it without breaking stride, barking orders as men scramble for weapons. Sabrina stands rooted for a second, her eyes locked on the enemy, before Tomas grabs her arm and pulls her toward the tree line.

"No," she says, her voice low and firm. "I'm not hiding."

She holds her ground, her fingers tightening around a curved dagger I'd almost forgotten she carried. I want to argue. I want her to hide, but there's no time.

The Spaniards charge. Steel hits steel. Boots thunder against wet earth. I slam into a man, parrying his sword and driving my elbow into his nose. He screams, his blood spraying, and I spin behind him, dropping him with a clean slice.

To my right, Cyrus is a whirlwind of fury, firing and reloading.

A cry splits the chaos, sharp and unmistakably hers.

"Sabrina!"

I snap around just in time to see her being dragged backward by a hulking man with yellowed teeth and a wild grin, his filthy hand wrapped around her throat, her feet kicking against the ground. Her dagger is gone, and he presses a rusted blade to her ribs, taunting in broken English.

"Pretty, eh? Coming with me."

My blood runs cold, then hot.

"Unhand her!" I surge forward, rage giving me speed. He pulls her tighter, the blade nicking her skin. She flinches, but her eyes find mine.

Suddenly, she knees him hard in the groan. He doubles over with a grunt but doesn't fully release her. I'm there in two strides, tackling him full-force, my shoulder slamming into his chest. We hit the ground hard, rolling. His blade misses my face, just barely. I drive the hilt of my sword into his skull. His eyes roll.

Sabrina drops to her knees beside me, one hand on my shoulder. "Gabriel—are you—"

"I'm fine," I rasp, my chest heaving. "Are you hurt?"

"No, I'll be all right." She's trembling, but unharmed.

Gunfire crackles behind us as more Spaniards storm the beach, but our crew meets them with fury. Isla hurls a rock into a man's temple. Tomas slices another's arm with a machete.

Smoke fills the air. The stench of powder and blood is everywhere. The surviving raiders attempt to flee to their boats, but my crew is relentless.

Cyrus drops the last man with a precise shot to the chest. Silence falls, broken only by the lap of waves and the soft moans of the wounded.

I hold Sabrina tighter, burying my face in her hair, the scent of smoke clinging to her like the memory of danger. "Never again," I whisper. "No one touches you. Not while I draw breath."

The world has tried to steal us from each other more than once, and it will try again, but for now, we're alive. We're together, and by God, I'll see her safely through any storm, no matter what it costs me.

RUMORS

Sabrina

The smoke still hangs low over the sand, curling like ghosts around broken crates and torn sails, and the air reeks of gunpowder and blood. I press a cloth to the cut on a sailor's arm, whispering something comforting even though my own hands won't stop shaking. Isla kneels beside me, tying a bandage with quick, practiced fingers around his leg.

"We got lucky," she murmurs. "There would have been more of them than us, if we'd met up with them at sea."

I nod, though nothing about this feels like luck. Men are limping. One is unconscious. A few will bear scars they didn't have yesterday, but we're all alive.

Gabriel paces near the boats, barking orders, keeping the remaining crew sharp while we get ready for departure. Tomas hauls a barrel toward the waterline, his face smudged with soot, his machete still tucked into his belt like he doesn't trust the danger to be over.

Gabriel hasn't left my side long. After he killed a man to save me, he helped drag the wounded back into camp. Now he stands ankle-deep in the surf, checking the ropes on our longboat, giving one last set of instructions to the men we're leaving behind.

We'll still sail back to Port Royal. We still have to warn the city before the earthquake. I sling a pack over my shoulder and make my way toward the water. Gabriel and I climb into the longboat, Tomas and Isla settle in beside me, and Cyrus steps in last. He sits with his rifle across his knees, his gaze scanning the shore one last time.

The crew left behind waves us off, with gold in their pockets and worry in their eyes. I wave back, my heart seizing, grateful they're loyal enough to Gabriel to stay.

Once aboard the ship, the breeze hits me hard and clean, chasing away the heat of battle. Our makeshift crew moves like clockwork, unfurling sails, checking rigging, adjusting course. I watch Hispaniola fade into the fog. We barely survived the island, and now we're sailing straight toward the storm.

Gabriel joins me on the quarterdeck, his hand brushing mine before settling firmly against the small of my back. I lean into him, his presence wrapping around me like armor.

When the sails are trimmed, and the last commands are given, he turns to me with a quiet look. "Come below."

I follow him through the narrow corridor into his cabin. The door clicks shut behind us, muffling the outside world. He turns to face me, his eyes searching mine.

"I could've lost you," he says, his voice low, hoarse.

"You didn't," I whisper. "You saved me again."

I reach for him at the same time he reaches for me, and then there's nothing between us, no doubt, no distance. His mouth finds mine in a kiss that's all fire, desperation, and promise. I clutch his shirt in both hands, needing to feel that he's real, that we're still here.

He lifts me, carries me the short distance to the bed, and we fall together into the soft chaos of tangled sheets and muffled moans. The world narrows to the slide of skin, the press of lips, the way his hands roam like he's trying to memorize me all over again, and I revel in it.

Gabriel's hands and lips are everywhere as he strips me bare, peeling away every scrap of fabric until my skin is flushed and trembling beneath his touch. His mouth finds my breasts, warm and demanding, his lips and tongue worshipping me. I arch into him, gasping as his teeth nip gently, the fire in his eyes matching the heat building deep inside me. Every kiss sends shivers up my spine, igniting a hunger I can no longer contain.

When he slides inside me, slow and steady, a sharp gasp escapes my lips. He fits perfectly, like he was made for me, and the rhythm of our bodies moving as one coils tight and wild. It doesn't take long before waves of pleasure crash through me, trembling in his arms. I feel him follow, locking us together in the fire of everything we've fought for.

When it's over, I lay my head against his chest, listening to his breathing. The ship sways gently, carrying us toward a city doomed to drown.

"I love you," I say. I need to say it. I might not get another chance.

His hand slides through my hair. "I love you," he murmurs. "No matter where that storm takes us, I'll always take care of you."

I close my eyes and let the sea carry us forward.

* * *

The wind stays steady and kind, filling the sails just enough to keep us gliding. Dolphins crest alongside us, or flying fish skim the surface like skipping stones through the calm ocean. The weather holds, and there are no sudden squalls or dark clouds creeping on the horizon. It's almost too perfect, like the sea is trying to lull us into peace before it strikes.

Each morning, I wake with Gabriel's arms still wrapped around me, the sound of waves tapping gently at the hull. We share quiet breakfasts with Isla and Tomas on the quarterdeck. Cyrus stands watch not far away, his eyes always scanning the horizon like it might betray us.

Our skeleton crew, just enough to keep the ship running, moves with silent efficiency. No complaints, no questions, just the creak of the ship, the soft slap of water against wood, and the occasional gull overhead.

We chart our course each morning, marking the crawl across the map with careful fingers. We'll arrive just in time, if the history books are right. If the timing is exact, we have three days before the storm hits.

I try not to think about it too much. I try to enjoy the sun on my face, the wind in my hair. I try to pretend, for a little while, that this is just a voyage. Just a ship. Just a man I love, but even in peace, I feel the pressure building.

Gabriel is quiet most of the time, but not distant. He stands behind me as I look out at the small waves, his hand brushing mine or settling at the small of my back. When he passes by me, he presses a kiss to my temple. He listens when I talk, even when I'm not saying anything that matters.

Cyrus sees land first, shouting it from the deck.

From a distance, the city looks unchanged: whole and alive. We reach the port, and the sails are trimmed, the anchor laid, and the ship eases into the harbor, slowing with the tide, gliding past merchant vessels and fishing boats.

We dock without trouble, and I release a slow breath, one hand tightening on the railing.

Gabriel steps up beside me again, his voice low. "We've got a few days."

I nod. "Taverns, shops, inns, anywhere people will talk."

"We spread rumors," he says. "Anything to drive them inland."

Isla joins us, her face pale but determined. Tomas steps up next, and Cyrus follows. The five of us stand there for a beat, looking out at the city that doesn't know it has an expiration date.

Port Royal is whole for now, but this is the calm before the storm, and we're the only ones who know it.

* * *

When morning comes, it's the light through the porthole that stirs me first, but it's Gabriel beside me, shifting in his sleep, and the whisper of his breath against my shoulder, that pulls me fully awake. When I glance back at him, his eyes are already on mine.

There's a plan to carry out and lives to save today. I know the clock is ticking, but for one moment, with Gabriel next to me, sunlight spilling across his handsome face, I wish we could stay in bed all day.

As the sun rises and the dock stirs to life, we gather below with the ones we trust most: Isla, Tomas, and Cyrus, faces still shadowed with sleep, but willing to carry out our mission.

"As I've told you all before, there's an earthquake coming. A tsunami," I say. "In two days' time, Port Royal will be destroyed."

Gabriel steps in then. "This isn't a hoax," he says. "It's a certainty. The Earth will crack. The sea will rise. Port Royal will be swallowed whole. We must warn the people of the danger."

Tomas curses under his breath. Cyrus mutters something that sounds like a prayer. But Isla nods slowly, then lifts her chin. "Start with the women and children."

Tomas runs a hand through his hair. "How do we get people to leave their homes without sounding mad?"

Isla turns to Tomas. "We tell them there's a sickness spreading. One that kills women and children. That it's already claimed lives."

I nod, heart racing. "People might ignore a storm. But a plague? That's fear they'll believe."

Gabriel adds, "We will also tell them there's treasure buried near Spanish Town, enough gold to tempt the worst of them."

Tomas exhales. "So we lie."

Gabriel nods. "Aye. We lie. The truth won't be enough."

No one disagrees. Isla steps forward, her jaw set. "Then we'd better start now."

We split up, moving through the sun-drenched streets of Port Royal as the city begins to wake. Market stalls open. Dockworkers haul barrels and crates, the smell of fresh fish thick in the air.

I trail Gabriel and the others as we spread whispers of plague, danger, treasure. I watch Isla speak calmly to mothers holding squirming children. I hear Tomas lean into the doorway of a tavern and warn of sickness in the air. I see the doubt in some people's eyes, but in others, I see fear.

Gabriel speaks with a group of fishermen by the shore, his voice low and steady. "Word is, there's gold buried out past the ridge," he says. "Spanish marks. Enough to sink your boat if you haul too much."

They laugh at first, but the hunger in their eyes gives them away.

Later, near the merchant square, I stand just behind him as he draws a small crowd, traders, dockhands, boys too young to shave. He spins his tale like a net and tosses it out.

A woman clutches her child tighter. A man with sunburnt shoulders narrows his eyes.

Gabriel doesn't flinch. "What's the risk?" he asks them. "A day's walk?"

The crowd murmurs. Slowly, they begin to drift off, and I step closer to him, brushing his hand with mine.

The hook is set.

By late afternoon, the mood in the city shifts. Doors slam. Horses are packed. Whispered rumors pass faster than any storm. It's working.

After spreading a few rumors myself, using my practiced English accent, I find Gabriel by the waterfront, watching ships sway gently in the harbor. "It's happening. They're leaving," I say softly.

He nods, but his eyes stay fixed on the sea. "Fear moves people, but greed moves them even faster."

We stand there as the sun drops lower, casting gold across the water. I can feel the gravity of the coming days pressing in, of what we're risking and what we're trying to save. More than anything, I feel the pressure of time. Of how little we might have, and how fast it ticks away.

Gabriel turns to me, his voice quieter now. "What if this is where our story ends? What if you're meant to go back, Sabrina?"

My throat tightens. "I don't know what's waiting for me back in my time, but I know what's here now. I know I'm meant to help."

His gaze softens. "I just don't want to lose you."

I step into his arms, pressing my forehead to his chest, feeling the pull of the future like an undertow, and I hold him tighter, so he can anchor me to this moment just a little longer.

EARTHQUAKE

Gabriel

I stand with the map spread across the table, tracing my finger along the path inland, away from the city, the sea, and away from impending doom. The Blue Mountain foothills are remote, and high enough to be safe from the waves. I tap the spot with finality.

"That's where you'll go," I say, lifting my eyes to Tomas, Isla, and Cyrus.

Tomas frowns. "You're not coming with us?"

I shake my head. "No. Sabrina and I still have work to do here. We will help get people to shelter, help the wounded. The three of you have done enough. I won't have you dying in a city we're trying to save."

Cyrus crosses his arms. "We ain't likely to tuck tail and run."

"No," I say quietly. "You aren't cowards. You're heroes. Some people have fled the city thanks to you. You've saved lives. Now save yourselves."

Isla glances toward the porthole, where the sky has begun to shift from copper to indigo. "How far?"

"A day's journey," I say. "I've arranged for horses and a guide. There's a Maroon village tucked in the trees. They won't welcome you at first, but show them this." I reach into the chest behind me and pull out a small silver medallion shaped like a breadfruit tree with a broken shackle dangling from its limb, given to me years ago by a man there who said he owed me his life. "They'll know I sent you."

I hand each of them a pouch of coin heavy enough to feed a dozen families, let alone three travelers. "This should cover whatever you need once you're there. Shelter. Supplies. Bribes, if it comes to it."

Tomas hefts his pouch with a grunt. "You paying us off, Captain?"

I smile, grim and tired. "I'm paying you forward. You've risked everything for Port Royal. Now, I ask you to take care of yourselves. That's all."

Cyrus mutters something under his breath but tucks the pouch and the map away. Isla, silent until now, steps forward and wraps her arms around me. She holds tight, longer than I expect.

"You better make it through this storm, Captain," she says against my chest. "You and Sabrina both."

I nod, throat tight. "We will."

Sabrina and I watch them mount up in the morning mist, the city waking behind them. They ride without looking back. We see the dust trail fade, the last glimpse of Isla's bright scarf vanishing. Tomas and Cyrus lead the way on horseback.

Sending them to the Blue Mountains was the right decision, but damn if it doesn't hollow me out, watching them disappear like that, as though the world's already ending.

Sabrina stands beside me at the rail of *The Tempest's Vow*, the wind tugging at her hair. The ship sways gently beneath us, anchored just outside Port Royal's harbor. The sea's quiet now, calm in a way that feels unnatural, like it's waiting.

She slips her hand into mine. "I've been thinking," she says softly, not looking at me. "If I stay with you in the city, I might end up going back home when the storm comes, and I've decided I want to stay here with you."

I turn to her, not sure I've heard right. "You mean—"

"I mean, I want to try to stay in this time with you," she says. Her voice is steady, but her fingers tighten around mine. "If the storm opens the doorway again... I want to resist it. I want to stay."

The breath leaves me in one long exhale. I hadn't let myself hope for that. "Sabrina—"

"You've saved my life more than once, and I don't want to spend the rest of it wondering what might've happened if I'd stayed. I don't know what's coming, but I know I want to face it with you."

For a moment, I don't speak. She's choosing me, not out of fear or necessity, but out of desire. I hold her face in both hands, pressing my forehead to hers.

She pulls back just enough to look into my eyes. "Then let's make sure we don't get caught in the city when it hits. We have one day left."

"Tomorrow's the seventh of June," I say grimly. "We find the fastest way out of the city today. Horses, a cart, or a pair of asses if we must. We'll spread the last of the warnings and be gone by dawn."

She laughs at my pun, and nods. "Then let's get moving."

I kiss her quickly and fiercely. "One more day," I whisper against her lips. "Then the storm."

By nightfall, we've secured a horse and cart from a stable hand who doesn't ask too many questions once I place a coin pouch in his palm and tell him it's a matter of urgency. The cart's old but sturdy, and the mare attached to it has strong legs and a steady gait, more than enough to get us out of Port Royal when the time comes. We leave the cart at the stable, packed and ready with food, water, and supplies. Sabrina insisted we wouldn't have much time to move, said the quake would strike mid-morning, and I believe her.

Tonight, we sleep, if only for a few hours. I hold her against me and listen to the sounds of the port one last time, the far-off whistles and hollers of drunk sailors, and the creak of ships in the harbor.

Before the sun set, we'd made one final circuit of the town, through the fish markets, the taverns, even the church steps, dropping whispers and warnings, the kind that spread faster than fire. Rumors of plague, buried gold, and even soldiers coming to seize the city— anything to make them pack and flee. I don't know how many will listen. I just know we tried, and come morning, when the tide shifts and the sky brightens over the bay, we'll be gone.

The sun's barely above the rooftops when we push into the streets, but the city's already buzzing. Too many people, too many carts, too much damn noise. I keep Sabrina close, my hand tight around hers as we weave through the crowd toward the edge of town, where the hired horses are waiting.

But they're not here. We turn the corner, and the stables are empty. No horses. No cart.

"They were supposed to meet us at the stables," I mutter, scanning nearby faces and alleyways. My heart pounds harder with each step. "Paid last night in advance."

Sabrina exhales sharply. "They're not here."

"No," I mutter. "They took the coin and ran."

I spin, taking her with me, dodging barrels and crates. Somewhere behind us, a vendor bellows about salted cod. A pirate curses someone for stepping on his dog. Everything feels louder, hotter, more intense than usual.

We try to find another cart, another horse, anything that moves, but everything's been bought or stolen. People are already fleeing, and most of them don't know why, not truly. Our whispered rumors of plagues and gold have people moving, and we're stuck.

The clock's ticking. I can feel it in my bones. The storm, the quake, it's coming, and we're still here.

Sabrina grips my sleeve. "Gabriel. What if we don't make it out?"

"We will," I lie. "We'll find another way."

We hurry back into the winding alleys, away from the port, the stink of fish and sweat heavy in the air.

"There," Sabrina gasps, pointing to an old mule cart rattling down the road.

I sprint after it, waving both arms. "Stop! We'll pay you—"

The driver whips the reins harder, and the cart lurches past us, one wheel wobbling. Gone.

I double over, breathing hard. Sabrina holds her arms over her head, gasping. "We're not going to make it out in time."

"We need to get off the streets," I say. "If we can't outrun it... we survive it."

She nods. "Where?"

I grab her hand again. "High ground. Something solid. Stone."

Sabrina runs ahead, weaving through the narrow lanes that wind toward the harbor's edge. I follow closely, sweat stinging my eyes as we push past vendors closing up stalls and sailors too drunk to notice the urgency around them.

Fort Charles rises ahead, its stone walls squat and weathered, the cannons pointed out to sea, but it's the highest ground we can reach, and we both know we're running out of time.

We sprint past the King's Warehouse, past the customs house, where an officer shouts something we don't stop to hear. The fort is only a few streets away now.

The sound comes first—not a crack, not a roar, but a deep groan from beneath the earth, like the island itself is in pain. I freeze mid-step, every hair on my body lifting as the ground shudders beneath me.

Then it hits, violent and sudden, the street lurching sideways like a ship struck broadside. Cobblestones split, walls buckle, and the bell in the chapel tower swings wildly before crashing down in a rain of stone and brass. Screams rise around us as buildings collapse like paper, and the sky itself seems to tilt. I grab Sabrina, pull her against me, and brace us against a crumbling wall.

This is it. The Earth is breaking apart.

Around us, mayhem unfolds in a terrible symphony of fear and destruction. Children wail, women scream, men curse and try to pull the fallen free, but every moment the Earth seems more unsteady, cracking open along the parade ground, where horses rear in terror, their hooves striking the fractured stones and sending shards flying.

A panicked stallion tears loose from its reins and barrels through the crowd, sending people sprawling, its hooves slick with mud. Screams rise from every direction as buildings behind me groan and shudder, bricks raining down like hailstones.

Sabrina's hand slips from mine in the crush of bodies and debris, and then she's gone, swallowed by the turmoil. I shout her name, but the roar of the earth, the cracking of stone, the shriek of horses and the crash of falling timber drown out my voice. Dust chokes the air, thick as ash, and I shove forward, coughing, searching, but I can't see her. I can't see anything but ruin.

I search desperately for Sabrina among the throng, scanning faces etched with disbelief and dread, but she is nowhere to be seen, drowned in the sea of fleeing townsfolk.

I call her name again, my voice raw and desperate. I help a man trapped beneath a collapsed wall, prying the timber loose with my hands. Pain and fear fill his eyes. Nearby, another man struggles, his body wedged beneath the crumbling ruins, his face streaked with tears and grime.

As I run to him, the sea answers the Earth's fury with a terrifying roar, a low growl rising from the harbor. I look toward the bay just in time to see the water retreating unnaturally, pulling back as if inhaling before it exhales disaster.

A great wall of water towers over the horizon, rushing toward the shattered city with merciless speed. Screams turn to howls of terror as the tsunami crashes through the streets, sweeping away carts, tossing boats like toys, washing away homes and people alike.

I fight against the tides of fleeing crowds, trying to hold my ground, trying to find Sabrina amid the bodies and collapsing city. The saltwater tears at my clothes, cold and biting, carrying with it the cries of the drowning and the desperate. I must dive into the water beneath a falling beam to avoid being crushed as the ocean's weight desecrates walls that stood moments before.

When I resurface, gasping for air, the streets I knew are gone, replaced by a chaotic flood of destruction and death.

Through the rising water, I scream Sabrina's name, every fiber of my being twisting with fear and hope. I push onward, clutching at anything–broken furniture, half-sunken barrels. I'm determined not to lose her to the storm's wrath, but as the flood rushes past, I see only frightened faces, shattered homes, and wreckage where the city once stood. Sabrina has vanished into the chaos.

I fight back despair and focus on pulling survivors from the water, hauling them onto whatever high ground remains—broken rooftops, half-collapsed walls, anything that can keep them above the merciless tide. I shout directions, help the injured crawl away from the rushing sea, but every moment, I'm searching for her. Sabrina's absence presses hard against my chest.

The storm has broken Port Royal, but it has not broken my will. As the waves finally begin to retreat, I vow with everything in me: I will find her. I will bring Sabrina back, no matter the cost.

HOMESICK

The moment Gabriel's hand slips from mine, my world becomes a nightmare. I scream his name, but the sound vanishes in the thunder of the Earth splitting apart. Crashing and roaring devour my voice.

People slam into me from every direction, all elbows and shoulders. A man barrels past with blood dripping down his face, clutching a bundle wrapped in cloth, and I pray it's not a baby he carries.

I try to fight against the tide, to push my way back toward where I last saw Gabriel, but the ground bucks beneath my feet like a wild animal. I hit the dirt hard and crawl toward the nearest wall as stones rain down from the collapsing buildings.

I scramble to my feet and push past a toppled cart. And there, the harbor is drained, the ocean pulled back in a black wave. Ships lie on their sides in the mud, and fish flip and gleam on the exposed bay floor.

I don't even have time to turn before the water, towering, pitch-black, and furious, punches the city like a fist. The sound is deafening, and the force knocks me back.

I'm tumbling, tossed like driftwood as water closes over my head. I try to yell, but it's useless, and I don't know which way is up. Something solid slams into my ribs. My arms flail.

I catch a glimpse of the sky before I'm dragged under again. The water tears at me, pulls my hair, rips my clothes, rakes across my skin with wood, glass, and stone. Then something cracks hard against the back of my head, and the world dissolves.

* * *

I wake choking.

The taste of salt clings to my lips. Sand coats my tongue. I roll to my side and vomit seawater. My whole body shudders. I cough, gasp, and finally force my eyes open.

I'm lying on the beach. White sand, palm trees, and the glass-fronted villas of my resort stand in the distance, shining like they always did.

No debris, no broken ships, and no people crying in the streets.

I push myself upright on shaky arms. My dress, what's left of it, is soaked and torn, stained with mud. My heart races, and I can barely breathe. I clutch my stomach, trying to remember, trying to make sense of the leap.

Gabriel.

I look around wildly, scanning the beach, the tide, the path leading back to the resort. There's no sign of him. No wreckage, no cobbled streets or burning buildings, just smooth concrete paths and perfectly trimmed hedges. I hear the faint hum of air conditioning from the nearby cabanas.

"No," I whisper. "No, no, no."

The storm brought me back, and not just out of Port Royal, but out of the past.

Back to 2025.

I curl forward, pressing my forehead to my knees, trying not to vomit again. The breeze is warm and full of the scent of coconut sunblock and the faint smell of grilled shrimp from the resort bar where the party goes on with no notice of my turmoil, but I feel dizzy and nauseated.

It's over. He's gone. I'm here, and he's still there, in that broken city, in the past, facing the end of the world.

The waves roll in gently now, as if nothing ever happened. As if the sea didn't just drag me across centuries and tear my heart out along the way.

The moment I stagger toward the resort entrance, the panic is already palpable. Voices call my name.

"Sabrina!"

I blink against the glare of the late afternoon sun, dizzy and soaked raw, and then I see her—Maddie, her face pale but full of relief. She's racing toward me across the polished stone walkway. Behind her, a small crowd of resort staff and a few guests gather, their eyes full of worry and confusion.

"Sabrina!" Maddie throws her arms around me before I can say a word. "Where have you been? We've been looking everywhere. The authorities came. They sent out a helicopter and search parties."

I want to tell her everything about the earthquake, the tsunami, Gabriel, the city crumbling, the chaos, the impossibility of it all—but my throat closes tight. The words feel too heavy, too crazy to utter. How can I explain any of it? How could they believe me?

Instead, I shake my head, my voice barely above a whisper. "I... I don't know. I was... somewhere else."

Maddie pulls back, her eyes searching mine. "You've been missing for hours. We got hit by that storm, and then we just lost you. You were just gone."

She hugs me again, and I swallow hard, the reality of it sinking in. For them, it was just a missing person case, a brief disappearance that ended in a miracle.

For me, it's been weeks... weeks of living through battle and water, of holding Gabriel's hand, of running through the streets of a city being torn in half. Of love and loss.

"How do you feel?" Maddie asks, worry creasing her brow.

"Confused." I close my eyes. "I feel... like I'm drowning."

Someone hands me a blanket. I wrap it tight around my shoulders, grateful for the warmth and the softness, but it does nothing to stop the tremor inside.

The others step forward now–a couple of staff members, a concerned-looking officer who says he's from the local police department. They ask questions—where did I go and what happened? I answer with vague, half-truths. I say I fell in the water and got separated from everyone, that the storm scared me, that I blacked out. Anything to keep the impossible at bay.

Later, after a doctor has assured us that I'm physically okay, Maddie sits beside me in the quiet of our room. "You scared me to death," she says softly, reaching for my hand.

I look at her, the woman who's been my rock through everything, and I want to confess, to tell her that I didn't just disappear and that I was somewhere else entirely, but the words choke me.

How do I tell her that time folded around me like a cloak? That I watched a city die, a man vanish, and somehow, I woke up here— where nothing has changed but I'm suddenly broken?

"If I told you what happened, I don't think anyone would believe me," I say instead, voice cracking. "Not even you."

Maddie's expression softens. "You probably hit your head. I'm just so happy you came back to me."

I nod, but inside, the doubt gnaws at me. Was it a dream? A hallucination? Some trick of the mind brought on by fear and exhaustion? But then I remember the dress, the one I was wearing when I washed up on the beach. It wasn't mine. Maddie didn't notice, thankfully, but it wasn't from the resort boutique or anything I'd packed in my suitcase. No, it was one of the gowns Gabriel bought me in Port Royal, made of hand-dyed fabric and tiny pearl buttons. I still have it, hidden deep in my luggage like a secret I can't let go of. No one in the twenty-first century made that dress, and I didn't dream up the feeling of Gabriel's hands on me or the way he said my name. I couldn't have.

That night, lying awake in the cool, sterile room, the memories flood back with haunting clarity. Gabriel's face, handsome and fierce, his hand slipping from mine as the Earth cracked open beneath us.

The roar of the sea, the choking dust, the desperate scramble for safety. The moment I was thrown into the water, and then the quiet, empty shore where I awoke.

Tears slip down my cheeks, hot and heavy. The pain of loss is almost unbearable. I'm here, but a part of me is still out there, lost in time.

* * *

The days pass with maddening slowness. I go through the motions. Maddie stays close, insisting I rest, eat, and try to have some fun, but how do I find joy when someone I loved so much has been ripped away from me?

I want to believe the world I saw was a dream, that the past is locked behind a veil I'll never cross again, but something deep inside whispers otherwise. The way Gabriel looked at me, the way the storm tore through us—it was all real. And yet, I must keep the story inside me, a secret wrapped in grief and hope.

I let Maddie pull me through the rest of our vacation like a shadow of myself. We sip cocktails by the pool, lay on sun-warmed loungers while some DJ plays beachy remixes I would've danced to weeks ago. We walk the shoreline, soft white sand curling over our ankles as the waves kiss the shore with perfect rhythm. I smile, I nod, and I even laugh sometimes.

But inside, I'm ash. Gabriel's face is burned behind my eyes. The shape of his smile. The rasp of his voice.

I wake up most nights with a gasp, my hand clutching the sheet where his should be. I dream of waves and stone streets. Of running. Of losing him again and again in the crush of the earthquake.

Maddie doesn't push. She just watches me sometimes when she thinks I'm not looking, her mouth pressed into a line. My best friend knows something happened to me. She just doesn't know what, and I can't tell her, especially when I barely believe it myself. And yet the ache never leaves.

We have two days left before our flight home, and Maddie suggests the museum.

"They have some pirate exhibit," she says, scrolling through her phone. "Artifacts from the island. It's air conditioned, and you won't have to smile at a bartender in a straw hat for two hours. Come on. You love this type of stuff."

The museum is tucked in a bright building with tiled floors and carved doors. Inside, the air smells of wood polish, and a docent greets us, handing Maddie a map. We walk through rooms of cannonballs and old flintlocks, of Spanish coins and clay pipes.

I turn a corner and freeze. In a glass case with a linen backdrop, there's a small bronze plaque beneath a pendant.

I step closer. It's silver, rough-hewn, and handmade... a broad, rounded disc shaped like a breadfruit tree, and hanging from a branch, a pair of open shackles. The silver is old and worn smooth by time, but the details remain—deliberate, powerful, alive.

I know this piece. Gabriel gave it to Tomas and Isla. He told them to show it to the Maroon villagers in the Blue Mountain foothills. He said it came from a man who owed him his life.

My knees nearly buckle as I read the plaque.

"Pendant, late 17th century. Believed to originate from a Jamaican Maroon settlement. The breadfruit tree symbolized sustenance and freedom; the open shackles suggest a history of resistance. Discovered in 1902 near the Blue Mountain foothills, remarkably preserved."

Maddie says something behind me, but I don't hear her.

It was real.

Gabriel, Tomas, Isla. The medallion, the storm, the earthquake. A sob catches in my throat before I can swallow it, and my fingers tremble as I press them to the glass.

I want to reach through and steal it. I want to shout that I loved him. Instead, I whisper, "I wonder if he lived through the storm."

Maddie appears beside me, her eyes wide, searching my face. "Sabrina?"

I try to answer, but my throat is raw. I just shake my head, blinking back tears furiously.

We finish the museum in silence, but I don't see anything else. My eyes blur everything into color and shadow, my thoughts tangled in time, waves, and memories.

Back at the resort, I pack my things. I fold my clothes, zip my shoes into the suitcase, and all the while, I try to imagine walking back into my apartment in New York as if nothing happened.

But it all happened. I fell in love with a man three centuries ago and watched a city drown. I lived through it, and now I have to go home without Gabriel.

The ache of that truth is something no amount of time or distance will ever wash away.

THE SABRINA

The city is quiet now, but it's not a peaceful kind of quiet. It's the silence after screaming that hums in your ears and presses on you like a yoke you can't lift.

Smoke clings to the bitter air, and the sea licks at the mangled shoreline with false gentleness. The same water that swallowed the streets now retreats in regret.

I move through the rubble, my shoulder throbbing with every step. Something must be torn beneath the skin, perhaps cracked. I felt it when I braced against a wall and caught the edge of a collapsing beam. My ribs ache from being thrown across the stone streets, and my legs are bruised and cut open in places I haven't even looked at yet. Alas, I still move, and I still search.

My voice is almost gone from shouting her name. "Sabrina!" The sound of it breaks something in my throat, raw and desperate. "Sabrina!" No answer.

Only the distant sobbing of a child, the coughing of a man dragging himself over wreckage, the sharp clatter of falling stone as yet another wall gives up and folds into itself.

I search the bodies I pass, my heart stalling every time I see curls or a familiar scrap of fabric. None of them are Sabrina, and I'm grateful that she's not broken and lifeless in the dirt.

Picking my way through what used to be the marketplace, I see the fish stalls are gone, shattered and washed inland with crates, nets, and the twisted corpses of boats. Dozens of men and women dig through the wreckage nearby, pulling out survivors where they can, and stacking the dead nearby. No one speaks unless they have to, for lack of vigor left for words.

I stop to help where I can, lifting and pulling. I wrap a gash on a woman's arm using my sleeve and press my hand to a lad's chest to feel the faint flutter of his breath. Then, I carry him to a patch of high ground, where a group is laying out the injured on dry patches.

And every time I turn in a new direction, I look for her. I search every alley, shoreline, broken doorway, and tumbled wall.

When the aftershocks come, I freeze, instinct tightening every muscle in my body. The ground shifts again beneath my boots, not as violently as before, but enough to remind us all that the Earth hasn't quite finished its tantrum. Cries rise around me. People flinch and clutch each other. Some drop to their knees in prayer. Others simply wait, hollow-eyed, for the next blow, but I keep moving.

There's a stretch of beach where the tide hasn't fully receded, and I walk the edge of it, ignoring the pain in my legs, my boots squelching through wet sand and broken city. I scan the surf for any sign of her. For a scrap of her dress, the sound of her voice, God forbid, her body. Anything.

The guilt is a living thing in my chest. I should've held her hand tighter. Should've shielded her better. Should've pulled her with me instead of letting her run ahead. I was right behind her. I swear I was, but then I wasn't, and now she's gone.

I stop walking for a moment as the sea whispers at my feet like it knows something I don't. I press a hand to my ribs and breathe through the pain. The sky above is smeared with ash and the low orange blood of a sun fighting through the smoke. Port Royal is dying behind me. It's crumbling, bleeding, and weeping, and still, I only yearn for Sabrina.

* * *

The next day.

The road to the Blue Mountains is slow going. My shoulder throbs with every step, my body stiff and sore from the bruises the quake left behind. The horse I ride is sturdy even on the narrow, winding trails that snake up into the green heights above the ruined city. Trees close in on either side, thick with heat and shadow, the air rich with the scent of wet earth and hibiscus.

I keep my eyes ahead, my jaw tight, my heart heavier than it's ever been. Every clop of hoof against rock takes me farther from the city where I last saw Sabrina, and yet there's nothing left for me there.

The Tempest's Vow is splintered and half-sunk against the harbor's edge, her rigging tangled in shattered dock beams, her sails shredded.

At twilight, the Maroon village greets me with suspicion at first, as expected, but when I tell them I know one of their own, and that I've come for Isla, Tomas, and Cyrus, they nod and step aside.

When I set eyes on the three of them gathered at the table of some kindly folk who've taken them in, hope stirs inside me. They're whole, alive, and breathing. For a brief moment, the harshness of the shattered world fades, and seeing them alive and unharmed is the only kindness I've found since the Earth tore itself apart.

"You're hurt," Isla says, rushing forward. She brushes my sleeve back to reveal the bruising beneath, but I wave her off gently.

"Not badly," I say. "And you three—you're safe?"

Tomas grunts. "We kept our heads down like you said, but we heard, Captain. About Port Royal. The quake and the storm. We heard about it all."

Cyrus looks me over. "Where's Sabrina?"

My silence answers for me. I see it land in their faces: Isla's eyes fill with tears, Tomas's expression hardens, and Cyrus lowers his head. No one says anything more.

We don't linger. The village offers us water and food, but I can't stay in those quiet hills, not when there's still something more I must do. Not when I made a promise to my crew—the men who follow me without question.

We ride down the far side of the range two days later and reach a coastal inlet that hadn't been touched by the storm just far enough east, sheltered by cliffs. There's a shipyard there, modest but standing, and a few merchant vessels moored in the calm waters of the bay. I use the last of our coin and trade a few personal items I never meant to part with for a ship that isn't much to look at. It's narrower than the *Vow*, and lower-slung, a brigantine with dull sails and weathered decking, but she floats.

Cyrus runs his hand along the gunwale and nods. "She'll do."

"We need a name," Isla says, quietly, as we load crates into the hold.

Alas, I can't bring myself to give her one yet. It feels like betrayal, naming something new while the *Vow* is still waterlogged and broken.

Before we sail, we make one final stop in a nearby port town, a place with market stalls and a crooked little tavern that gets word up and down the coast faster than any printed sheet. I press coin into the barkeep's hand and tell him what to say.

"If a woman named Sabrina passes through– tall, honey eyes, curls to her waist–tell her we've gone to Hispaniola. Tell her to wait here, that we'll come back for her."

He nods. "You have my word."

We leave that night, the wind filling the sails with a low groan. The stars are clear above the water, and for the first time in days, I feel like we're moving toward something, not just running from the wreckage.

But I can't shake the ache in my chest. I've lost the ship I re-built with my own hands. I've lost the woman who changed everything. The only thing left is the oath I made to my crew, the men stranded on Hispaniola. I'll get them back, just as I promised, and then I'll keep searching for her.

Even now, with the wind at our backs and the sea opening before us, there's a part of me that refuses to believe she's truly gone.

Just before dawn, the stars fade, and the horizon glows gold, casting the sea in molten light. We've cleared the last of the reefs off the Jamaican coast, and the sails are full and quiet. I stand at the helm, one hand on the wheel. Tomas leans against the rail beside me, his eyes on the horizon.

"You going to name her?" he asks, voice low.

"Sabrina," I say finally. "She's called *The Sabrina*."

Tomas nods once, like he expected that. "Then she'll sail strong."

She does. We reach Hispaniola within days, and the men we left behind are camped near the inlet where we promised to return. The moment they spot us on the water, they raise a shout that echoes across the rocks, as if they knew it was us before they even saw our faces. Cyrus helps them aboard one by one, as I stand back and let them reunite, the men who followed me into storms and bloodshed, who trusted me when I said I'd come back.

Once the crew is settled, we turn back toward Jamaica, our sails fat with wind, the men laughing again. There's a bit of life among them still.

When we return to Port Royal, what's left of it, the air smells of smoke and sea rot. The city sounds different. Streets that once roared with trade and vice now echo with the sound of hammers and saws. The dead have been burned or buried, the wounded carried off to the hills. Those who remain are building, grieving, surviving. Most of my crew scatters, some to Spanish Town, some deeper inland where the ground feels steady again.

I berth *The Sabrina* just outside the harbor, in the shallows where the water's clearest, and I make a camp near the cliffs overlooking the old docks. There's nothing left of the *Tempest's Vow* now but a few blackened ribs of wood sticking out of the surf like bones.

Each morning, I rise before the sun and walk the beach, scanning the shoreline for signs of her. Sometimes, I see a flash of movement across the waves, and I bolt to my feet, my heart hammering. Sometimes, I swear I see her in a crowd—just a shape, a gesture that reminds me of her—and my lungs stop working.

Tomas visits once. He brings supplies and a fresh shirt, and he watches me with the same concern I see in the eyes of the townsfolk who pass me on their way to rebuild the city.

"You still think she's coming back?" he asks, not unkindly.

"I don't think," I say. "I believe."

Tomas just nods and says nothing more. He presses a hand to my shoulder and walks away.

Nights are the hardest. I lie on the deck of *The Sabrina,* staring up at stars that no longer comfort me, remembering her voice, soft in the dark. I remember the feel of her breath on my neck.

I don't know how many seasons will pass before I see her again. Spring may bloom and fade, summer may blaze, and autumn may fall, but I'll keep searching.

The storm took her from my arms, but I'll follow every whisper of wind, every shift in the tide, until I find the path she traveled. I know what we had was real, and if the storm carried her through time, I'll learn how to chase time itself.

SURRENDER

Taxi horns blare through the din of the city, weaving beneath the chatter of pedestrians barking into phones and the ever-present wail of sirens slicing through the humid summer air. We step off the airport shuttle and into the gray smear of New York, the sky above thick with clouds that never seem to break. Around me, people move forward in a relentless tide, their eyes fixed ahead, their shoulders hunched with purpose.

I stand still for a moment, just long enough to become an obstacle, the kind people mutter about under their breath as they jostle past. The concrete beneath my feet is familiar, but it feels strangely hollow now, like a stage set.

I should feel comfort in this chaos. The noise, the energy, the sharp, unyielding rhythm of this city that always made me feel so alive. Feelings of home fade, and they are replaced with a world I've outgrown.

My shoes click against the pavement as I walk, and every sound echoes sharper than it should, bouncing off the glass and steel of the buildings that rise like sentinels on either side. The streets smell of hot asphalt, car exhaust, and the faint, greasy promise of food carts lined up outside subway entrances. I know this city's ebb and flow, the way the light hits the crosswalk signs, the exact timing of the traffic lights near my apartment, but I don't recognize myself here anymore.

I grew up here, and I love this place. When I was in Port Royal, I missed New York's pace, pulse, and familiarity. I missed my museum with its endless quiet corners and chilled air that smells like old paper and lemon polish.

My nameplate still waits for me at the archival wing of the Metropolitan Museum of History. Megan, the receptionist, greets me with a squeal and open arms, and I smile like I'm happy to be back. Like I belong here.

But everything feels off-kilter now. The walls are too clean and the lighting too sterile. My desk is just as I left it: notes tucked under paperweights, a cracked teacup filled with pens, the exhibit schedule half-highlighted, but it feels like someone else's life.

I sit at my computer and stare at the blinking cursor for five full minutes before I can even type my password. I should be thrilled to be here. Weeks ago, when I first fell into 1692, I would've done anything to reclaim this rhythm, this certainty. Climate control, coffee runs, Tuesday night trivia with Maddie and the group.

Now, I long for sea-salt air in my nose, the creak of *The Tempest's Vow* beneath my feet, and especially for Gabriel's hand closing over mine when the world shakes.

I walk the museum floor on my break, hoping the exhibits will comfort me like they used to. They were my sanctuary, but now they're a torment. Each display taunts whispers of lives long vanished: colonial glassware, maps of trade routes, emblems of rebellions. I pause too long in the Caribbean wing, staring at an etched compass with rust along its edge and a sextant that reminds me of one I saw in his quarters. My reflection in the glass is pale and stretched thin. I barely recognize her.

At home, my apartment is cold, tidy and untouched, like it never missed me. I make tea and forget to drink it. The books I once devoured sit unopened on the shelf. I scroll through my phone and wonder how I used to find any of it interesting.

People ask where I went, and what happened while I was missing. I lie, mostly by omission. I say I needed time, or the storm gave me temporary amnesia, or that I hit my head and disappeared for a while.

No one questions it too deeply, but no one knows I dream in cannon fire and cobblestone streets. That I wake up reaching for a man who isn't there. That I shudder every time I see the ocean, as if it might pull me under again, drag me backward through time to the moment I lost him.

Summer turns into autumn and then winter. The city blurs around me, headlights and wind, music from bars. I used to crave this noise, and now I'd give anything for the chirp of jungle birds at dawn, clatter of hooves, and the rough warmth of his callused hand catching mine. My heart still beats for a man left behind in a world that's crumbled to ash.

* * *

Three years pass.

I don't mean to let them, but then I blink, and somehow I'm twenty-eight. I still live in the same apartment, walk the same streets, and work the same job, but the girl who once curled up on this couch watching period dramas, or went out with Maddie for trivia and beer for fun, doesn't live here anymore.

She drowned with Port Royal.

Most days, I function on autopilot. I dress the part, give lectures on artifacts, argue with curators about grant budgets and humidity levels. I smile at my colleagues, send birthday cards, but underneath it all, I'm still looking. Quietly, obsessively, and endlessly searching for any sign of Gabriel.

Not a day has passed that I haven't thought about him and wondered if he made it. Prayed that he did.

For the first year, I scoured shipping manifests and colonial records during every spare moment. I tracked mentions of the *Tempest's Vow* in dusty maritime registries and handwritten port logs from Kingston, Nassau, and Hispaniola. I ordered microfilm from private archives in England and Spain and squinted through reel after reel until my eyes blurred and my neck seized up. But Gabriel Ashford doesn't leave much behind. Not officially, anyway.

The Tempest's Vow appears in a few port entries in the late 1690s, listed as a merchant vessel out of Kingston under a G. Ash—then nothing. The ship vanishes, like so many others lost to piracy, storms, or war.

I almost gave up twice. Once, after my grant application for Caribbean colonial tracking was denied, and again after I spent a small fortune on an auctioned captain's journal that turned out to be a forgery, but something keeps pulling me back.

Then one afternoon, as winter light slices across my desk, and I'm buried in a box of miscellaneous acquisitions from an estate sale in Saint-Domingue, I find it.

It's not much, just a brittle piece of parchment folded into quarters, tucked behind a moldy handkerchief and a cracked compass. There's no official label, no date, no fanfare, but the moment I unfold it, my heart stops.

It's a letter, water-stained in ink so faded I have to hold it to the light to read.

March 1694

To the gentleman who inquired after Captain Ashford—he sails no longer under English colors. He commands a brigantine, name unknown, though he was once the captain of The Tempest's Vow. *Last sighted trading goods off the northern coast of Hispaniola. I advise caution—he travels with a massive crew, which include Maroon allies, and he carries no flag, bows to no king.*

I stare at it for a long time, afraid to breathe.

He lived!

The earthquake didn't kill him. The sea didn't take him. Somehow, against all odds, *he survived.*

I read the letter again, whispering the words aloud like a prayer. "He commands a brigantine... once the captain of *The Tempest's Vow....*"

My hands tremble so badly I have to set the page down before I ruin it. I stand, pace the room, press my palms to my face, and let out a mixture of a laugh and a sob.

He *lived,* and if he lived, maybe he kept searching, too. Maybe he's out there still, wondering if I made it. Looking for signs in the sky. Watching the waves for something, *anything,* to bring us back together.

The thought undoes me, and I sink to the floor, my knees pulled to my chest, that little piece of history, *our* history, spread out on the rug beside me.

For three years, I've been a woman out of time, caught between two centuries, two versions of myself, but this could change everything.

Gabriel Ashford is not just a memory. He's a man who survived the fall of a city. A man who never flew another flag but his own. A man I once loved—still do—and I'm going to find him, even if I have to pass through time itself again to get there.

* * *

The letter, now safely encased in an acid-free sleeve in my desk drawer, is sealed into my thoughts. I stare at maps, tracing shorelines with trembling fingers. Where would he anchor? Where would he trade?

Although it's not just the letter I can't stop thinking about. It's the *storm.* That's what carried me away the first time. A tempest that cracked time wide open. A violent, unnatural force that bent the rules of the universe and dropped me into a city on the brink of collapse.

So I start watching the weather, and I download apps meant for sailors and meteorologists. I track pressure systems and wind currents. I bookmark the NOAA hurricane tracker and watch every swirl of cloud that forms off the coast of West Africa. Most fizzle out or drift harmlessly north, but every now and then, one moves west with a fury I can feel in my bones.

The first time I see one, a hurricane, I feel a pull deep in my chest. The storm is days out, predicted to brush the Caribbean before swinging north toward Florida. I book the flight to Kingston that night.

It's madness. I know it is. Who flies into a storm? If I'm wrong, I'll come home bruised, windblown, and maybe even a little humiliated, but if I'm right... I could find him, and that makes it worth it, even if I don't return at all.

I write the letter the night before I leave, which takes me hours. I start it three times and tear each version into pieces, but I owe Maddie the truth. After everything we've been through, after all the questions she never pushed me to answer, she deserves to know, and if I disappear for good, this will be the only way she ever will.

By the time I finish, my eyes are swollen from crying. I fold the pages carefully and slide them into the envelope. I write her name on the front, and below it, in smaller letters: *Please don't open until September 12.*

That gives me five days. Five days to fly into the storm, walk the shoreline, and hope time cracks open again. Five days to make it back to Gabriel.

The next afternoon, I ask Maddie to lunch. We sit outside, under a polka-dot umbrella, sipping sangria and sharing shrimp tacos like we've done a hundred times before. She talks about work, and I listen, nodding, but I already feel a thousand miles away. She doesn't know this is goodbye forever.

I memorize everything about her all over again. This woman has been my anchor, my sister, my sanity. I hate lying to her, but I don't know how to explain that I'm about to try to leap through time on a wish and a storm surge.

"Maddie," I say softly. "Promise me something."

She eyes me warily. "Okay... what?"

I pull the letter from my bag and press it into her hand. "Don't open this until the twelfth."

She frowns. "Sabrina—"

"I mean it. Please. No matter what, just wait."

She holds the envelope, studying my face, worry creases her brow. "Is this one of those 'if something happens to me' things?"

I swallow the lump in my throat. "Kind of. But nothing bad is going to happen to me. Just... trust me, okay?"

She nods slowly, still frowning. "I do. You know I do."

I stand first, hugging Maddie tight. I breathe her in, letting the familiar shape of her center me one last time.

"I'll see you soon," she says.

I nod, and it's the biggest lie I've ever told.

"Yeah," I whisper. "Soon."

But I know I won't. If this works, if the storm pulls me through time again, I'll never stand on this sidewalk, in this city, in this year, ever again. My life here with Maddie will end. My new life will belong to another century, and when she reads the letter, when she finally knows everything, I hope she understands.

I don't pack much, just a satchel with my passport, and the dress I wore when I woke up on the beach three years ago, the one from Odette's shop.

The flight is rough. Turbulence rattles the cabin and sends drinks sloshing across tray tables. I close my eyes and grip the armrests, half from fear, half from hope. Maybe this is how it starts. Maybe this is the first pull of time letting go.

I land in Kingston just after sunset. The wind is already rising, tugging at palm trees and sending fine grit skating across the asphalt. People are moving fast, taping up windows, buying batteries, stocking water. The airport announces closures for the following day.

"Lucky you," the cab driver says sarcastically as he winds through the streets. "You got here just before the worst of it."

I nod, my heart thudding. "Yeah. Lucky."

He drops me at a small bed-and-breakfast not far from the coast in Port Royal. The woman at the desk checks me in. "You'll want to stay inside tomorrow," she says. "The waves get high when the storms come. Power goes out, too."

I thank her and climb the stairs, but I don't plan on staying inside.

The wind howls all night. I lie awake with the dress in my arms, staring at the ceiling fan as it wobbles in its mount. The storm builds in my chest like an echo.

By morning, when the storm is supposed to be at its peak, the sky is a bruised violet, and the air buzzes with static. Rain lashes the shutters, and then the power flickers and dies.

I pull on the dress, button the front, and slip down the stairs. I pass through the dark lobby and walk out the back door into the wind. Branches whip overhead, and trees bend like dancers in a fever dream.

The shoreline is empty, the sky roaring above me, a churning mass of black clouds split by veins of lightning that crawl like fire across the heavens. The ocean gnashes and seethes, hurling itself against the jagged rocks in violent gushes, foam flying like teeth. Rain slashes sideways, soaking the linen of my dress until it clings to my skin like ice. My hair whips across my face, stinging my cheeks, tangling around my mouth.

"Take me back," I whisper, my lips trembling. "Please. Take me back to him."

The storm doesn't answer with peace or promise. It answers with rage. A thunderclap splits the sky so violently I flinch, my ears ringing. The ground bucks beneath me, slick and trembling. I stagger, my arms flailing. A gust slams into my chest with enough force to knock me to my knees. I gasp as my palms scrape the stone, and when I lift my head, the world is spinning.

Then something hits me hard. A branch? A piece of debris? I don't know. It slams into my ribs, knocks the breath from my lungs, and I collapse flat against the rocks, coughing, dazed. Pain radiates through my side, and for a second, I can't move.

What if this was a mistake?

The thought pierces like a blade. *What if I was wrong? What if this storm doesn't take me back—what if it kills me?*

The fear is sharp and sudden, curling cold fingers around my throat. I force myself up onto my elbows, the rain running down my face. Lightning strikes somewhere behind me, close enough to blind, and the air smells like sea rot.

I try to breathe through the pain. "Gabriel," I whisper, my voice breaking. "Please."

Another wave slams against the rocks, higher this time, swallowing my legs. Water rushes over me, freezing and full of force, dragging me forward a few inches before receding. My nails dig into the stone.

I'm shaking, soaked, bruised, and completely alone, but I don't give up. The wind screams louder, shrieking like it's trying to rip the world in half again.

Goosebumps prickle as the air feels charged. Then, a roar rises from between the sky and the sea. From everywhere all at once, and when the waves surge like a massive wall, I see it coming, and I don't scream. I close my eyes and surrender.

Something cracks inside me or around me—I can't tell—and all light vanishes.

THE SEARCH ENDS

Gabriel

The wind off the bay tastes of brine, tar, and fish from the dockside stalls. I lean against the railing of the ship, my boots planted wide as the tide laps at the hull, and scan the harbor through narrowed eyes. Another ship comes in, her sails furled, the crew calling to the men onshore. I watch, but she's not on this one either.

"Still waiting like a dog at the door," Isla murmurs from behind me, hands on her hips, her voice laced with quiet sympathy. "You know the odds, Gabriel."

I do. I've heard them muttered behind my back more times than I can count. *The captain's gone mad. Still chasing ghosts. Should've taken another woman by now. Should've moved on.*

But they don't understand. They didn't love her like I did. Like I still do.

"I keep watch because if she can slip through time twice, she can do it again."

Isla doesn't argue. She just sighs and moves along, the wood creaking beneath her feet as she joins Tomas near the gangplank. My crew is fiercely loyal, and together, we've seen it all, but I haven't seen her in three years.

Every port we anchor in: Kingston, Nassau, Hispaniola, the Caymans, I ask. I pay informants and pass messages through the old trade lines. I've interrogated priests, merchants, and brothel madams. I fought two men who dared to falsely claim they'd seen her and meant to profit by it.

Alas, I've nothing to show for it but the echo of her voice in my dreams. We took to the sea again after Port Royal split open and drowned half the damned city, but I swore I'd never stop looking. I never stay gone long. No matter how far we sail, or who we fight, I always come back here. I've scoured every corner of the Caribbean in search of her, and I still keep coming back.

The remainder of my crew reinforced and rebuilt my new ship with no flags and no mercy for those who prey on the weak. We move through the Caribbean like smoke, vanishing into coves and inlets the English Navy doesn't even know exist.

And still… my sails pull me back to the ruins of this city like a compass to true north. Every time we return, I check with the keeper at the rebuilt inn, the older woman at the river bend who trades herbs and hears every whisper of gossip before it leaves a man's mouth, and the barmaid, Rosa, who had her place back up and running mere months after the storm.

Today, we sail back to Port Royal from a trade trip up the coast of the island of Cuba. One moment, the sea is calm, and the next, wind slices through the rigging of *The Sabrina*, sharp as broken glass. The sky splits open with a crack of thunder that shakes the masts.

"Reef the topsail!" I shout, rain already driving into my face like needles. "Drop the main before she rips loose!"

The crew scrambles to obey, running across the slick deck, their hands working fast and furiously through the ropes. Tomas vaults onto the quarterdeck, already yanking down sailcloth while Isla curses the lightning darting across the clouds like veins of fire.

I've sailed through worse. Squalls off Tortuga, tempests off Hispaniola, but something about this storm feels different. It's not just weather. It's personal, like Mother Nature is angry.

The sea bucks hard beneath us, waves rising like fists. *The Sabrina* shudders but holds fast, as she always does. Built for speed and storm alike, and loyal as any beast I've ever known, she was born from wreckage and rage. I named her for the woman who changed me and vanished like a dream.

Rain stings my lips, and my coat is soaked through. Lightning turns the world bone-white for a heartbeat, and in that flash, I see the broken skeleton of Port Royal's ruins in the distance, half swallowed by the sea, half rebuilt by desperate men. My hands grip the wheel tighter.

"She's holding!" Tomas calls from the bow, his voice nearly lost in the wind. "Another push like that, and we'll clear the reef!"

We ride the wave like a phantom, *The Sabrina* cutting through the water with deadly grace. She takes a beating, but she never breaks.

When we reach the cove just past the shallows, the wind starts to fall off, abrupt and eerie. Rain still falls in sheets, but the edge has gone out of it. The sky lightens by a degree as though the worst has passed.

I brace against the wheel, listening to the sea groan under us. The crew moves around me, securing lines, catching their breath.

We dock just beyond the market path, and I disembark before the gangplank even finishes lowering. It would take a storm like this to bring her back to me.

The streets are flooded, the windows of makeshift houses shuttered tight. I'm heading toward the tavern when a young lad tears down the road, his boots sloshing through the water, his arms pumping hard. He skids to a stop in front of me, panting, his eyes wide.

"Captain Ashford!"

I nod once, wary. "Aye."

He shoves wet hair out of his face and thrusts a hand toward the tavern road. "You need to follow me, Sir. Rosa says it's urgent."

Rosa's the one who's kept her ears open for me these last three years, the one who passes on every strange whisper, every tale of time and storm.

"What is it?" I ask. "What's happened?"

The lad shakes his head, his breath still ragged. "I don't know, sir. She just said, 'Fetch Captain Ashford as soon as he docks.'"

My pulse quickens. "Is Rosa hurt?"

"No, no—it's not like that," he says quickly.

My blood goes cold. I start moving, my legs already picking up speed. Ahead, the tavern is small and familiar. We reach the door, and I rush inside.

Lamplight glows against damp wood. A few people look up, but they don't speak. They part for me like the sea splitting open.

Rosa waits near the hearth, and her gaze meets mine with something I've never seen in her before. It's not a warning, not curiosity, but quiet, reverent awe. She doesn't say a word, just nods toward the back room.

I feel every second of the last three years in my bones—every unanswered question, every letter written with nowhere to send. Every night I stood at the edge of the sea and begged the storm to take me, too. I've imagined this moment in a thousand ways: awake, dreaming, drunk. But I never dared believe it would come.

The door to the back room is open just enough to see the shadows dancing along the wall. I push it the rest of the way, slowly.

And there she is.

She stands by the far window, her back to me, soaked to the skin in that same dress she wore the day I lost her. Her hair drips down her spine in curling tangles, darker with rain. Her shoulders are shaking, but she's upright, whole, breathing.

She turns slowly, and her eyes find mine instantly. In a moment, the room falls away. The wind, the sea, the years between us vanish.

Her lips part. "Gabriel."

My name from her mouth wrecks me.

I cross the room in two strides and stop just in front of her, close enough to touch. There are bruises blooming on her arms, a cut at her temple, and her ribs rise too fast, like she hasn't stopped shaking since the storm hit.

"I thought I was dead," she whispers. "I thought it didn't work."

I raise my hand slowly, afraid she'll disappear if I move too fast.

My fingers skim the edge of her cheek, warm despite the storm, and my throat tightens to the point of pain.

"You didn't die," I say. "You came back."

Her voice cracks. "It's been three years."

"I know."

"I tried everything. I waited. I searched—"

"So did I. I never stopped looking for you, Sabrina."

She closes her eyes, and tears slide down her cheeks. "I was so afraid you didn't make it."

"I made it," I whisper. "And in all these years, I've never given up on finding you."

As I pull her into my arms, she buries her face in my chest. I hold her tighter than I've ever held anything or anyone. Her body fits against mine exactly as I remember. The rain still clings to her skin, to her hair, but she's here. Flesh and bone, heart beating, and I don't think I've ever known what it means to be grateful until this moment.

I rest my chin on her head. My voice is rough when it finally breaks free. "You came back to me."

"I had to," she says, muffled against my chest. "There wasn't a life without you in it. I tried. I really tried."

I draw back just enough to see her face again. Her lashes are wet, her mouth trembling, but her eyes, those bright, brilliant eyes... they're still the same.

I brush her hair away from her forehead and stare at her like I might never get to again. "I don't know how you found your way back through a storm," I murmur. "But I swear to God, I will never let you go again."

"I believe you," she says. "I always have."

Sabrina is here now, real, warm, breathing against me, and for the first time in three years, the ache in my chest subsides. I don't know what will happen next, what storm or shore lies ahead, but I know that she came back, and what time we've been given, I'll spend it beside her, thankful for every moment.

MYTHS AND GHOSTS

I chose love. I stood in the rain and let the storm take me because something in me knew it would carry me back to Gabriel. I don't know how long it will last, but I know I'm staying. This time, I'm not going back. I won't waste another breath pretending that I belong in a world without Captain Gabriel Ashford.

My boots slide in the mud as we walk side by side toward the docks, the sky still low and battered with the remnants of the storm. I steal a glance at him, at the face I missed so much. His dark eyes scan the harbor with quiet intensity. His jaw is shadowed with stubble, his features sharp and striking, still impossibly handsome in that way that made my heart skip from the very first moment.

When we round the corner, and the harbor comes into view, I stop short. The ship, his ship, is waiting, moored in the cove, her sails furled tight, her dark hull gleaming wet from the rain, and painted in clean letters across her bow is a name that steals the air from my lungs.

Sabrina.

I press a hand to my heart, which has started to ache in the most beautiful way. He built something new out of the wreckage of what was lost and gave it my name. I don't know what to say, and for once in my life, I don't try. I just look at him, he looks back, and the moment holds every promise we made three years ago. Gabriel smiles, and I walk with him hand in hand, down to the pier.

The gangplank is lowered, and the crew leans over the railing to get a better look. Isla is the first to recognize me, her eyes huge and bright. She lets out a whoop of laughter so full of disbelief and joy that it makes me laugh, too. She barrels toward me and nearly knocks me off my feet with the force of her hug, swearing loudly as she pulls back to look me over.

"You're soaked through and bruised and look like you fought the storm itself," she says, "and by God, I've never been happier to see anyone in my whole damned life."

Tomas is right behind her, taller now and broader in the shoulders, but still the same boy in the way he blushes, grins, and looks at me like he doesn't know what to do with all the emotion in his heart. I pull him into a hug, too, because I missed him more than I can ever explain.

Then Cyrus is here, his hair longer and streaked with more silver, but his eyes are as sharp as ever. His voice is quieter than the others but thick with emotion as he says, "Took your time, did ya, lass?"

I laugh again, blinking back tears because it all feels so impossible and so perfect at once. They surround me, the crew I once sailed beside, the people who became my family, and I see shock, joy, and welcome in every face. Three years have passed, but it might as well have been yesterday for the way they draw me back into the fold without question.

That night, the ship sways beneath us, anchored just beyond the edge of the harbor, the lanterns swinging gently with each pull of the tide, casting honey-colored light across the cabin walls. Everything feels dreamlike—the creak of the wood, the low murmur of the waves, the whisper of my own heartbeat as Gabriel closes the door behind him, and the world outside disappears.

He doesn't speak at first. He just looks at me like I'm still not entirely real, like I might vanish with the next gust of wind, and I understand because I feel the same way. We're standing on the other side of a miracle, suspended in a moment we both prayed for, and now that we're here, it's as fragile as it is fierce.

I reach for him first. My fingers find the hem of his shirt and slide upward, my palms pressed to the warm skin of his abs, and then he pulls me into his arms, but nothing's rushed or frantic.

When he kisses me deeply, I melt into him, and it feels like coming home after wandering for too long in the dark. We move toward the bed without speaking, our clothes slipping away one piece at a time, and when we finally lie tangled together in the hush of the cabin, there's nothing between us but love.

He touches me like he's grateful, like he still can't believe I'm real, and I hold him like I've been waiting forever. The world outside falls away–the years, the storms, the time that swallowed us whole. And in this moment, there is only this: skin on skin, breath against breath, the weight of his body over mine, the way he says my name like a prayer he never stopped whispering into the sea.

Later, we lay in silence, my head on his chest, his heartbeat steady beneath my cheek.

"I thought I'd forgotten the sound of your voice," he murmurs into my hair, his breath warm against my temple. "But the moment you spoke, I remembered everything."

"I never forgot you," I whisper. "Not once. Even when I tried."

He pulls me closer, and I feel it in every part of me—the depth of our love and the way it's been stitched into the very fabric of time. We don't know how long we have, but tonight, we have each other.

* * *

Years pass. Not in flashes, but in golden, sun-drenched days and storm-tossed nights, miles traveled and maps rewritten. In salt-rimed sails, moonlit harbors, and in the steady heartbeat of a life I never could have imagined but somehow got to choose.

I sail beside him, my captain, my match, my home. *The Tempest's Vow* is gone, buried with the broken bones of Port Royal, but *The Sabrina* lives, and so do we. Gabriel stands at the helm with the wind in his hair and fire in his eyes, and I stand beside him with my charts and my ink-stained fingers, a compass always hanging from my belt.

In my old life, I was a historian. I documented lives, traced them in brittle ledgers and faint handwriting. Pieces of people who were long gone were filed away as I tried to shape stories out of the wreckage they left behind. I thought that was enough, that knowing the past was the closest I could come to meaning, but now I understand that history doesn't live in archives. It lives in choices, in risks, in love and fear. It lives in bodies, breath and the sound of your name on the lips of someone who waited three years for you to come back from three centuries away.

We become a story, the two of us. Not all at once, not in the loud way some legends are born, but over time, through whispers passed over rum bottles and campfires, through songs sung in harbors and marketplaces. A woman from nowhere, with knowledge no one can explain. A captain who never bowed to a crown, who carved out his own compass and followed it wherever it led. A crew as loyal as any kingdom's guard. We never fly a flag, but the name *Sabrina* becomes both a warning and a wonder.

We fight when we must, we help where we can, we steal from slavers and trade and fight with freedom fighters and we run goods for Maroon settlements tucked into the hills where no army dares go. We listen to the warnings told by elders. Sometimes, I wonder if I was always meant to land here, not as a scholar but as a witness, not to preserve the past but to shape it.

And we love. In stolen minutes below deck and slow mornings in unfamiliar ports. In letters scrawled on scraps of paper when we're separated for more than a day, in fights that burn hot but end in laughter, in the quiet moments when he holds my hand and says nothing at all—because he doesn't have to. The world changes around us, but we move like shadows just beyond its reach, always a few steps ahead.

In the stories now told in Kingston and Nassau, on the wind-swept beaches of Tortuga and whispered through back-alley taverns where sailors trade truth for coin, we are more than real. We are myth. The captain who waited. The woman who came from another time. They say I can read the weather better than any man born beneath this sun, that I speak languages never heard on these shores. They say Gabriel commands the sea itself, that his ship appears and disappears like an apparition, always watching, always listening.

What they don't say, what they can't know, is how ordinary our love is in the quiet moments. In the quiet moments where I brush the hair from his brow while he sleeps. In the quiet moments where he leaves me peeled oranges in the morning when I wake after he's already left for an errand. In the quiet moment every night where he asks if I will choose him again in the morning, and every night, I say, I will.

I always do—and I always will… until the end of time.

Thank you for reading! Book 6, Back to the Inquisition, *will be out in September of 2025!*

ALSO BY ID JOHNSON

Stand Alone Titles

All I Want for Christmas is Pooch

(*sweet contemporary romance*)

Christmas Memory

(*sweet contemporary romance*)

Meet Cute Me Under the Mistletoe

(*sweet contemporary romance*)

The Doll Maker's Daughter at Christmas

(*clean romance/historical*)

Pretty Little Monster

(*young adult/suspense*)

The Journey to Normal: Our Family's Life with Autism (*nonfiction*)

Found by the Alpha (fantasy romance)

Love Throughout Time

(*time travel romance*)

Back to Titanic

Back to Gettysburg

Back to Bunker Hill

Back to the Highlands

Back to Port Royal

Back to the Inquisition (Sept 2025)

Back to Salem (Oct 2025)

Back to Plymouth (Nov 2025)

Back to Whitechapel (Dec 2025)

Back to the Old West (Jan 2026)

Back to the Ton (Feb 2026)

Back to the Crown (March 2026)

Back to Pompeii (April 2026)

Silverwood Academy

(paranormal romance)

Vampire Hunter

World Builder

Realm Jumper

Celestial Springs

(psychological thriller/literary fiction/women's fiction)

Beneath the Inconstant Moon

The First Mrs. Edwards

Leaving Ginny

The Motherhood

(dystopian romance)

Rain's Rebellion

Rain's Run

Rain's Return

Ashes and Rose Petals

(contemporary romance/retelling of Romeo and Juliet and Cinderella)

Girl in the Attic

Girl From the Tomb

Girl On the Beach

Nashville Country Dreams

(contemporary romance)

Meant to Marry Me

Lead Me Home

You Are the Reason

Forever Love series

(clean romance/historical)

Cordia's Will: A Civil War Story of Love and Loss

Cordia's Hope: A Story of Love on the Frontier

The Clandestine Saga series

(paranormal romance)

Transformation

Resurrection

Repercussion

Absolution

Illumination

Destruction

Annihilation

Obliteration

Termination

A Vampire Hunter's Tale (based on The Clandestine Saga)

(paranormal/alternate history)

Aaron

Jamie

Elliott

Christian

The Chronicles of Cassidy (based on The Clandestine Saga)

(young adult paranormal)

So You Think Your Sister's a Vampire Hunter?

Who Wants to Be a Vampire Hunter?

How Not to Be a Vampire Hunter

My Life As a Teenage Vampire Hunter

Vampire Hunting Isn't for Morons

Vampires Bite and Other Life Lessons

Gone Guardian

Death Does Not Become Her

Blood of the Vampire Hunter (based on The Clandestine Saga)

(paranormal romance)

Night Slayer

Shadow Stalker

Queen Catcher

Mother Hunter

Father Finder

Ghosts of Southampton series

(historical romance)

Prelude

Titanic

Residuum

Lusitania

Heartwarming Holidays Sweet Romance series

(Christian/clean romance)

Melody's Christmas

Christmas Cocoa

Winter Woods

Waiting On Love

Shamrock Hearts

A Blossoming Spring Romance

Firecracker!

Falling in Love

Thankful for You

Melody's Christmas Wedding

The New Year's Date

Charles Town Brides (based on Heartwarming Holidays Sweet Romance)

(Christian/clean romance)

From This Moment

Can't Help Falling in Love

It's Your Love

When You Say Nothing At All

My Girl

Unchained Melody

I Only Have Eyes For You

At Last

The Very Thought of You

Reaper's Hollow

(paranormal/urban fantasy)

Ruin's Lot

Ruin's Promise

Ruin's Legacy

When Kings Collide

(steamy historical romance)

Princess of Silence

Princess of Hearts

Collections

Ghosts of Southampton Books 0-2

Reaper's Hollow Books 1-3

The Clandestine Saga Books 1-3

The Chronicles of Cassidy Books 1-4

Celestial Springs Collection

Heartwarming Holidays Sweet Romance Books 1-3

Heartwarming Holidays Sweet Romance Books 4-7

Websites: https://books2read.com/ap/xX7ZD8/ID-Johnson

For updates, visit www.authoridjohnson.blogspot.com

Follow on Twitter @authoridjohnson

Find me on Facebook at www.facebook.com/IDJohnsonAuthor

Instagram: @authoridjohnson

Follow me on Bookbub: https://www.bookbub.com/authors/id-johnson

www.ingramcontent.com/pod-product-compliance
Lightning Source LLC
Chambersburg PA
CBHW060312310726
48976CB00007B/2305